'I thought some...
to you,'

she cried, aware tha........ .. .. eyes. 'I thought you were dead!'

'Hey, you really are upset, aren't you?' Sam looked down at her with a look of puzzled concern on his face.

She looked up into his face. 'If anything happened to you I really don't know what I'd do. I used to believe the unthinkable couldn't happen. But it did happen once and I know it could happen again...and quite honestly I don't think I could bear it...' Her voice cracked.

'Oh, Maggie.' Stepping forward, he took her hands, then drew her up into his arms and held her close in a warm hug.

'Thank God you're safe, Sam.' Her voice was shaky. She felt intensely aware of him, of the beating of his heart, the slight roughness of his jaw, the very maleness of him. Once again Maggie felt the stirring of some emotion deep inside—that half-forgotten emotion once known as desire.

Dear Reader

A Very Tender Practice is my thirtieth Medical Romance™ for Harlequin Mills & Boon®. For this reason, for its setting I have chosen to return to the Isle of Wight, which I have used for several of my books in the past. The Island is very dear to me, for not only was I born and bred there—and indeed still live there with my husband—it is also a place of great natural beauty, and with its gentle pace of life perfectly lends itself to a background for romantic novels.

I feel that thirty novels is something of a milestone, and by sharing this fact would like you to celebrate with me.

I hope you enjoy reading about the lives of the doctors, staff and patients in *A Very Tender Practice*—I certainly enjoyed writing about them.

With best wishes

Laura

A VERY TENDER PRACTICE

BY
LAURA MacDONALD

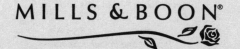

MILLS & BOON®

All the characters in this book have no existence outside the imagination of the author, and have no relation whatsoever to anyone bearing the same name or names. They are not even distantly inspired by any individual known or unknown to the author, and all the incidents are pure invention.

First published in Great Britain 2002
Harlequin Mills & Boon Limited,
Eton House, 18-24 Paradise Road, Richmond, Surrey TW9 1SR

© Laura MacDonald 2002

ISBN 0 263 82718 6

Set in Times Roman 10½ on 12 pt.
03-0202-52947

Printed and bound in Spain
by Litografía Rosés, S.A., Barcelona

CHAPTER ONE

'COME in, Fiona, please. It's time we had a chat. I'm sorry it's been so frantic since you arrived.' Dr Maggie Hudson pushed the unruly mass of her dark hair back from her face and indicated a chair alongside her desk. 'I would like to be able to say it isn't usually like this, that today is a one-off, but I'm afraid if I did I would be lying. It's always hectic here.'

'That's all right.' Fiona Winn, the new practice manager at the Downsfield Road Medical Centre, wrinkled her nose as she sat down. 'I've been talking to the girls in Reception but it's all rather confusing, especially as everyone seems to know everyone else—not just the staff but the patients as well.'

'It's like that here.' Maggie smiled. 'You're new to the Isle of Wight, aren't you?'

Fiona nodded. 'Yes, I was living just outside London until recently and, as you know, I was employed as manager in a large group practice in Chiswick.'

'So why the Island?' asked Maggie curiously.

'My parents live here,' Fiona replied. 'They retired to Seaview. I became disillusioned with the rat race so they persuaded me to give it a go here.'

'You'll find it very different from London, living here. But let's try and fill you in on some of the background here at the centre. Now, let's see.' Maggie opened a folder on her desk. 'You met my other two partners, Sam Neville and Jon Turner, at your interview, didn't you?'

'Yes, that's right,' Fiona agreed. 'And, if you remember, Dr Leonard Ward was also there. I understand that he was one of the founder members of the practice.'

Maggie nodded. 'Leonard's officially retired now, although he still does locum for us these days, but, yes, it's true that it was he and my late husband, David, and Sam Neville who founded the practice. I was busy having babies at the time. I've joined the practice since, first on a part-time basis but now, since my husband's death, I'm full time.' She faltered slightly as she always did whenever she mentioned David. It was over a year now since his death and while there were some days when she felt she was beginning to get her life into some sort of order, at other times she still felt swamped by her emotions.

'I'm so sorry about your husband,' said Fiona. 'I gather he was very young...'

Maggie took a deep breath, thinking it would perhaps be best to get everything out of the way at the start with this young woman who would be playing an important role in the running of the practice. 'It was cancer,' she said quietly. 'Inoperable. He fought bravely for fifteen months but he knew the score. We all did. He died just over a year ago. He was thirty-seven.'

For a moment Fiona looked quite stricken, as if she didn't know what to say next. 'Your children...?' she managed to say at last.

'Jessica is eleven and William is eight,' Maggie replied, her voice firmer now as she spoke of her children. 'They miss him dreadfully but life has to go on...' She paused. 'While we're on the subject of children, Sam Neville also has two children, a daughter of nine and a son, Richard— he's twelve—but they live with their mother.'

Fiona looked up quickly. 'Is Dr Neville divorced?'

'Yes, he and his ex-wife, Claire, parted four years ago.

I think it's important that you know these things to avoid any embarrassment.'

'Of course,' Fiona murmured. Casually she flicked back her blonde hair. 'And your other partner, Dr Turner—is he married?'

'Heavens, no. Mind you—' Maggie felt a smile tug at the corners of her mouth '—that's not for the want of trying by the local girls and especially by the various receptionists and nurses that we've had here. But our Jonathan just won't be tied down and I'm afraid he's got himself the reputation of being a bit of a heartbreaker.'

Fiona smiled back, and Maggie rose to her feet. 'I think perhaps I'd better leave the intrigues of the rest of the staff until another time. Now, if you'd like to come along to the office, I'll introduce you to Moira Silsbury, our secretary, who will sort out all your details concerning salary and tax and things like that. Later we're having a meeting,' she added, 'so that you can meet the rest of the staff.'

Together they left Maggie's consulting room and walked along the corridor to the secretary's office where, after the necessary introduction, Maggie left Fiona with Moira. It was while she was on her way back to her room that Sam came out of his consulting room. Sam, with his warm brown eyes and dark hair which somehow always looked tousled as if he was constantly at odds with the elements, was a couple of years older than Maggie.

'Maggie.' His smile echoed the warmth in his eyes. 'I was coming to see you. Has the new PM arrived yet?'

'Yes,' Maggie replied, 'I've just taken her down to Moira.'

'What time is this staff meeting?'

'Midday.'

Sam groaned. 'I thought so.'

'Bad time for you?' Maggie frowned.

'You could say that. Although I'm not sure what would be a good time today. After surgery I have a list of house calls as long as your arm, a meeting at two with Social Services, an antenatal clinic at three-thirty and a surgery at five.'

'Not what you'd call a rushed day, then.' Maggie smiled. 'I bet I could cap it.'

'Yes, I'm sure you could.' With a rueful grin Sam ran a hand over his dark hair. 'To be honest, Maggie, I sometimes wonder how you cope with it all—the practice, your patients and the children. I just hope you aren't overdoing it...'

'Not at all.' Maggie spoke briskly. 'I need it, Sam. You know that.'

'Yes, I know you do, but even so... I do worry about you, Maggie.'

'You mustn't. Really, Sam, I'm fine and, besides, I have Ingrid.'

'Ah, yes.' Sam nodded. 'The intrepid Ingrid. How is she?'

'As magnificent as ever, and the children obey her—which is nothing short of miraculous.'

'They're probably terrified of her,' said Sam dryly. 'I confess I am.'

'Nonsense. They adore her and, even better, she adores them. I have to say I'm truly blessed to have Ingrid.' Maggie gave a little sigh. 'I realise that when I hear the others talk about their problems with child care.'

'At least that's one thing I have to be grateful to Claire for,' said Sam with a rueful grimace. 'She does care for the children.'

'Ah, but Claire doesn't have to work—there is a difference, Sam.'

'Yes, I suppose so,' he agreed. 'And let's face it, she doesn't need to work—not with Luke Tyler's millions.'

Maggie was aware of a sudden pang of sympathy for this man who was such a good friend to her. So good, in fact, that she had no idea how she would have coped without him, especially since David's death. They had all been friends in happier times, she and David and Sam and Claire. Their children had been born around the same time and had played together as toddlers, but then Sam's and Claire's marriage had begun to flounder and eventually Claire had left Sam, taking their children, Richard and Emma, with her. It had been a bad time for Sam, and Maggie hoped that she and David had helped by standing by him and being there for him especially when Claire went on to marry Luke Tyler, a wealthy property developer.

'So what's she like, then?' Sam's voice dropped conspiratorially. 'This new practice manager?'

With a quick look up and down the passage Maggie shooed him into her room, following him inside and shutting the door behind them. 'She seems all right…but you saw her at the interview.'

'Yes, I know. But you can't really tell at interviews. People aren't themselves. They're either on their best behaviour in the hopes of impressing or they're so nervous they present a completely false image.' He paused. 'She's single, isn't she?'

'Yes, if by that you're asking whether she's married. She may, of course, be in a live-in relationship but we didn't get that far. She seemed more interested in all the low-down on us.'

'Really? I hope you didn't tell her too much.'

'Only the truth.' Maggie shrugged then she frowned. 'What shouldn't I have told her?'

'Well, I don't think there's a normally married one amongst us. Sorry, Maggie.' Sam's voice softened and lightly he touched her arm. 'I didn't mean you. But the rest of us, well, we're all either divorced or cohabiting. And then there's Jon…he's something else. I hope you warned her about Jon?'

'I did.' Maggie pulled a face. 'Of course I did. I felt it my duty. I would feel it my duty to warn any unattached female about Jon.'

'We're not sure she is unattached.'

'No…that's true.' Maggie wrinkled her nose. 'There's Aimee,' she said suddenly.

'Aimee? What about Aimee?' A puzzled look came into Sam's dark eyes.

'Well, she's married with three children. You said there wasn't a normally married one amongst us.'

'Ah, yes, Aimee. I forgot. Well, thank heavens for Aimee.' His eyes crinkled at the corners. 'So you think she'll do, then, this Fiona what's-her-name?'

'Fiona Winn. Yes, I think she'll do. She had very good references from her last employers.'

'Hmm, London practice, wasn't it?' Sam began fiddling with the folders on Maggie's desk.

'Yes, Chiswick.'

'She'll find this very different, what with all the temporary residents.'

'The summer's over and the visitors have nearly all gone. We practically have the place to ourselves again,' Maggie replied firmly. 'I only thought that today when I was driving along the Military Road and I hardly met another car.'

'So she'll find that different as well,' Sam replied dryly. 'The absence of traffic. It could take some getting used to after Chiswick! Where's she living?'

'She has a flat here in Millbury, but apparently her parents live in Seaview. I think she'll be all right, Sam. We'll just have to give her a chance.'

'Well, time will tell.' He shrugged.

'Did you have reservations at the interview?' Maggie studied his face carefully.

'A few,' he admitted. 'But, as you know, I'm not fully convinced that we need a practice manager anyway, and if we have to have one I'm not certain Fiona Winn is necessarily what we are looking for.'

'You should have said,' Maggie protested. 'I thought you were quite happy with the choice.'

'She was the best of the applicants…' He shrugged again. 'Still, like you say, we have to give her a chance.' He glanced at his watch. 'This won't do. I must get on or I'll never get through. See you later, Maggie.'

'Yes. Oh—Sam?' she said as he turned to go.

'Yes?' He paused in the doorway and looked back at her.

'Care to come over later for a bite of supper?'

'I'd love to. Thanks, Maggie.'

After he'd gone Maggie sighed and turned to the window. The medical centre was in an old building on the outskirts of the small town of Millbury situated in the west of the Wight. Maggie's consulting room was on the first floor and looked out over part of an estate of new bungalows. Behind the bungalows, rolling acres of farmland were dotted with rounded bales of corn and beyond that, if she stood on tiptoe, a glimpse of the sea could be seen—a single strip of silvery blue glittering in the morning sunlight. When David was alive they used to love to walk by the sea, whether on fresh spring days when clouds raced across the sky, darkening the waves beneath, or in winter when the surf crashed against the cliffs.

Together with the children and their two dogs they would walk for miles. At first, after his death, she could hardly bear to do the same but lately she had found solace in her walks.

With a sigh she turned away from the window and sat down behind her desk, preparing to start her surgery. She switched on her computer and cast her eye through the neat bundle of patient records which receptionist Katie Jones had placed there, together with her morning post.

Her heart sank as she saw that her first patient was a woman by the name of Jasmine Hyde. She had been treating Jasmine for a long time for irritable bowel syndrome. The problem was that no sooner had Jasmine started on a course of treatment than she would read about some other form of treatment, or one of her friends would suggest something which she thought would be better than what Maggie had prescribed. She would abandon the prescribed medication, start on the alternative and usually suffer side-effects from that, causing her to stop taking that remedy also. Only then would she wonder why her condition flared up again.

Maggie pressed the buzzer on her desk, and as she sat back to await her first patient she found herself going over her conversation with Sam concerning the new practice manager. It had come as something of a surprise to learn that Sam had been uneasy about Fiona Winn's appointment. Sam was usually an excellent judge of character and in the past Maggie had always trusted his judgement implicitly, so this latest revelation was a little disconcerting.

She was jolted from her reflections by a knock on the door. 'Come in,' she called, and the door opened to admit Jasmine Hyde. 'Jasmine.' Maggie half rose and indicated a chair. 'Please, come in and take a seat.'

Jasmine was a thin, anxious woman of around forty years of age. 'Good morning, Doctor.' She didn't smile as she lowered herself onto the chair.

'How may I help you, Jasmine?' asked Maggie, knowing full well what was coming.

'That last lot of tablets you gave me...'

'Yes, Jasmine. Did they help?'

'No. Not at all. If anything, I've been worse. Pain. Constipation. Diarrhoea.'

'How long did you take them for?' asked Maggie.

'Oh, only a couple of days. They weren't doing any good, so I stopped taking them. I couldn't see any point in carrying on with them.'

'You don't think if you'd persevered a little longer it might have given them a chance to work?'

'I shouldn't think so.' Jasmine shook her head gloomily. 'Anyway, I've seen these advertised.' She began rummaging in a large bag that she carried on her shoulder then produced a cutting from a magazine and passed it across the desk to Maggie.

Dutifully Maggie scanned the cutting. 'Well, if these tablets do what they claim, there should be some very happy people around,' she said at last.

'That's what I thought.' Jasmine nodded. 'So will you prescribe them for me, please, Doctor?'

'I'm sorry, Jasmine, I can't,' Maggie replied, folding the cutting and handing it back.

'But I can't afford them,' Jasmine protested. 'They work out at over twenty pounds for a month's supply.'

'I'm not allowed to prescribe them.' Maggie shook her head. 'They are only available from health-food shops— they are what is known as alternative medicine but I'm afraid they aren't available on the health service.'

'But it sounds as if they're very good. There are letters

here from people who have tried them and felt much better afterwards.'

'That may well be the case,' Maggie replied. 'But it doesn't alter the fact that I'm unable to prescribe them on the NHS.'

'Well, I think that's ridiculous. After all, if they're going to do good and the tablets you prescribed weren't any good at all—'

'You don't really know that for sure, Jasmine. Two days really isn't long enough.'

'So what am I going to do?' Jasmine stared at her indignantly. 'I can't afford twenty pounds a month. On the other hand, I can't go on like this.'

'Have you been keeping to the special diet I worked out for you?'

'Well, sort of, although it's been a bit difficult just recently. I had to go to a wedding and then I went for a meal with the people I work with—'

'Jasmine.' Maggie took a deep breath. 'I suggest you have another try at the medication I prescribed for you. I also suggest you try your utmost to keep to the diet. I know it's difficult and I do sympathise, but it will be for the best in the long run.'

'Oh, all right...I'll give it another go,' said Jasmine reluctantly. 'But if it doesn't work I'll be back.'

I dare say you will, thought Maggie as Jasmine left the room. She pressed the buzzer. The next patient turned out to be an elderly gentleman by the name of Percy North. Percy had worked on the land all his life and had retired fifteen years previously. He still, however, tended his large garden and he and his wife kept hens and sold fresh eggs, vegetables and flowers.

'How are you, Percy?' Maggie indicated the chair for him to sit down.

'Dreadin' the winter,' said Percy, removing his cap.

'Hopefully that's a little way off yet,' Maggie replied.

''Twere really autumnal this mornin',' he replied darkly. 'Thick dew first thing, probably afore you were up.'

'Yes, Percy, I dare say it was,' said Maggie with a laugh.

'Y'see, I gets this business where me fingers goes white—something to do with a fox you said it was.'

'A fox…?' Maggie frowned. 'Oh, you mean Reynaud's disease?' she said as she realised to what Percy was referring.

'Yes, that were it.' Percy nodded. 'Bloomin' nuisance it is when I'm tryin' to do me garden.'

Maggie checked Percy's medication chart on her computer screen. 'I see I gave you some tablets last year for this,' she said. 'Did they help at all?'

'I spose they must 'ave done.' Percy scratched his head. 'It cleared up.'

'We'll try them again, Percy.' Maggie typed in a command and waited as the computer printed out his prescription. 'Come back and see me if they don't help. And don't forget to have your flu jab this year. Now, tell me, how's Daisy?' she added as Percy took the prescription from her, folded it and carefully put it away in a battered leather wallet.

'Not so bad, considerin'.' He nodded. 'She said to tell you we have some produce for you.'

'That's very kind of you, Percy.'

'I'll drop it into Mill House later today.'

'Thank you, Percy.'

That effectively concluded Percy's consultation but it seemed Percy himself had other ideas for he made no attempt to move. 'How's Dr Ward keepin' these days,

Doctor?' he asked after a moment. 'I heard in the Post Office that 'is arthritis had been playin' up recently.'

'He's not too bad at present. I'll tell him you enquired.' Maggie smiled and nodded and with that Percy hauled himself to his feet and, after pulling on his cap and bidding her a solemn farewell, made his way out of her consulting room. It was quite true what Fiona had said about everyone knowing everyone else in this small community. It was good in some respects because it meant that people kept an eye on each other, but it also meant that everyone knew everyone else's private business.

After she'd completed her morning surgery Maggie made her way to the staffroom where she found several other members of staff already congregating for the staff meeting. Practice nurse Dawn Prentice had just arrived and senior receptionist Jackie Price was pouring coffee for them both. Jon Turner, the junior partner, was standing by the window, reading through a medical journal. He looked up as Maggie came in, then tossed the journal onto the low table in the centre of the room.

'Maggie. There you are.' He was his usual immaculate, handsome self. While totally aware of his appeal to the opposite sex, he was also completely at ease with it.

'Will this meeting take long, Maggie?' Dawn looked up, her expression anxious.

'Shouldn't think so.' Maggie shook her head. 'We just thought it important that everyone should meet Fiona officially. Isn't that right, Jon?'

'What's that?' Jon had turned away to talk to eighteen-year-old receptionist Katie who had just come into the room, but he turned back to Maggie as she addressed him.

'I was just saying that we felt it important that Fiona is welcomed properly and meets all the staff right away.'

'Oh, absolutely.' Jon ran his hand through his hair

which, bleached by the summer sun, flopped across his forehead.

At that moment Fiona herself entered the room, accompanied by Moira. 'Fiona,' said Maggie, 'come and take a seat. I'll pour you a coffee.'

Maggie crossed the room and while she was pouring the coffee she turned to Katie. 'Katie,' she said quietly, 'have you any idea where Dr Neville is?'

Katie frowned. 'His surgery ran late, but I thought he'd finished.'

'Would you like to slip along to his room and remind him of the time?' Maggie kept her voice low so that the others wouldn't hear. It wouldn't do for Fiona to think that the senior partner had forgotten this meeting.

As Katie sped away Maggie took Fiona's coffee across to where the new practice manager was sitting in one of the easy chairs. 'How has your morning been?' she asked.

'Confusing,' admitted Fiona. With a short laugh she uncrossed her long slender legs as she took the mug from Maggie. 'But give me time—it doesn't usually take me long to get to grips with things.'

'Dr Hudson?' Jackie was at her elbow.

'Yes, Jackie?'

'May I have a quick word about a patient while we're waiting?'

'Of course,' Maggie replied. 'Who is it?'

'Audrey Attrill—her X-ray result has just come in. I think you might want to contact her.'

'Very well. Thank you, Jackie. Leave it on my desk. I'll phone her…or, on second thoughts, I may call in and see her.' Maggie glanced up as the door opened and Katie came back into the room, followed by Sam.

One glance at his face told Maggie that he had indeed forgotten this meeting. To anyone else it would appear that he had merely been delayed by one of the many things that delayed doctors in the course of a busy day, but Maggie knew otherwise.

'Sorry to have kept you all.' He spoke briskly but courteously. 'As you know, the purpose of this meeting is to introduce and welcome our new practice manager, Fiona Winn.' He turned to Fiona and she inclined her head in response. 'We run quite a tight little ship here, Fiona, but I like to think it's a happy ship and we hope you also will be happy.' He looked round at the others. 'Fiona comes to us from a busy London practice, and while we have more than our fair share of hectic days I think she will find Island life very different from what she is used to. I hope you will do all you can to help her to settle down and adjust to this different way of life.'

There were murmurings from the others then Fiona stood up. 'Thank you, Dr Neville, for your kind welcome. Yes, I've no doubt I shall find life very different from the Chiswick practice, but I'm sure with everyone's help I'll soon learn the ropes here.'

'Fiona, I don't think you've met everyone yet.' Maggie moved forward, sensing that Sam had no more to say. 'This is Dawn Prentice—Dawn is one of our practice nurses. The other is Aimee Barnes, but Aimee is off sick at the moment.'

Fiona shook hands with Dawn then turned to Maggie again as she carried on with the introductions.

'Jackie and Katie you've met, and our other receptionist, Holly, is downstairs, manning the reception desk. There are two health visitors who call in each day and, of course, the community nurses. You'll meet them all later, but I think you've now met all the immediate members of staff.'

'All I have to do now is remember everyone's names,' said Fiona with a grimace.

Each member of staff had a brief word with the new manager and gradually as they finished their coffee they began to drift away until in the end Maggie found that she and Sam were the only ones left in the staffroom.

'You forgot, didn't you?' she demanded accusingly under her breath as she sidled up alongside him.

'What?' He frowned in an attempt at nonchalance and it might have worked if Maggie hadn't seen a tiny pulse at the corner of his jaw—a sure tell-tale sign that Sam was trying to get away with something.

'This meeting,' she persisted. 'You forgot about it.'

'No...' He shrugged. 'No, I didn't. Of course I didn't. I just got a bit sidetracked, that's all. I had some calls to make...a couple of referrals to do, e-mails to check and—'

'You forgot.'

'Oh, well, yes, I suppose I did,' he admitted at last with a reluctant sigh. 'Did anyone else notice?'

'I don't think so.' Maggie grinned. 'I think they all thought you'd simply been delayed. But I knew.'

'I sometimes think you know me far too well.'

'Maybe I do, but I guess that's pretty inevitable when two people have known each other as long as we have...'

'True.' Sam nodded then he paused. 'And I guess if the roles had been reversed I would have known the same about you,' he added.

'Well, there you are, then.' Maggie laughed. 'I don't see any harm in that.'

'Well, no,' Sam agreed. 'But you have to admit,' he added after a moment, 'it's also a bit scary—knowing someone as completely as that and also knowing that they know you just as well.'

'Yes,' Maggie said slowly, 'I guess it is.'

It was true, she thought as Sam left the room, they really did know each other very well. In fact, if she was honest, she supposed she now knew Sam almost as well as she had known David. Not in an intimate way, of course, but in little everyday things like the one that had just happened—in gauging his moods and his reactions to certain situations. And sometimes, in an uncanny way, they even seemed to know what the other was thinking— just like she and David had.

But that was where it ended, she thought with a little sigh as she rinsed her coffee-mug and made her way out of the staffroom and along the corridor to her consulting room. Sam might be her best friend but David had been her husband and now he was gone. She sometimes wondered if she would ever share that depth of love and understanding with anyone ever again.

CHAPTER TWO

'YOU must remember to drink plenty, Albert, especially whilst you're on this medication.'

'Never thought I'd hear you say that, Doc.' Albert Morrison managed a weak smile in spite of the pain he was suffering from his kidney complaint.

'I don't mean pints of bitter either,' Sam replied.

'I thought that would be too good to be true,' said Albert with a grimace.

'You need lots of water to flush your kidneys right through.'

'I've got lemon barley, Doctor,' Albert's wife Ethel chipped in. 'Will that do? He doesn't like drinking a lot of water.'

Sam glanced over his shoulder at Ethel who was hovering in the bedroom doorway. 'Lemon barley is fine, Ethel. And make sure he takes his tablets. He has a condition called pyelitis and I'm prescribing two different kinds of medication. The capsules are antibiotics to kill the bug and the others, the flat white tablets, are painkillers. Now, are you going to be able to get this prescription today?'

Ethel nodded. 'Yes, thank you, Dr Neville. My son, Brian, said he'd call in on his way home from work. He'll take it into Newport to the duty chemist.'

'Very well.' Sam scribbled his signature, tore off the page and handed the prescription to Ethel. 'Keep warm, Albert, get plenty of rest and you should soon be feeling a lot better.' He stood up and followed Ethel out of the

21

bedroom. 'If there are any further problems, give us a ring but, like I say, there should soon be an improvement.'

'Have you finished now for the day?' asked Ethel as she preceded Sam down the stairs and opened the front door.

'Just about.' Sam nodded. 'And I can't say I'm sorry, Ethel. It's been one of those days.'

'I thought you were running late.'

'Yes, I am,' Sam agreed. 'But yours is the last visit. I think I've earned my supper now.'

The sun was sinking beyond the distant mainland coastline, the sky flushed to a deep crimson and the sea darkening as Sam left the Morrisons' farm cottage and took the coast road home. He just about had time to shower and change before driving over to Maggie's for supper. He was glad he was going. He could relax at Maggie's and it really had been a brute of a day. If he was honest, Sam hadn't slipped easily into his role as senior partner— it was a role he had never envisaged or wanted. David had been roughly the same age as him and it had been inconceivable that he should die when he had. Sam had always imagined that he and David would retire at around the same age, with David remaining in the senior position throughout their working life.

He was fine with his patients. It was the administrative side of things he loathed, like today and the fuss over the arrival of the new practice manager. If he could just tend to his patients he would be happy, but it seemed increasingly of late that he was being called upon to make one decision after another, usually about things like staff holidays, disputes over pay or building repairs at the surgery—nothing at all to do with the welfare of his patients. Maybe things would change with Fiona Winn's appointment. The last manager they'd employed had been an older woman who'd worked part time and had only really dealt with the financial side of things. Fiona would, no doubt, be very different from that.

He drew into the drive of his house and switched off the car engine. The house, in shadow, loomed dark and silent before him. He should sell it really. It was too big now that he was on his own but he had wanted to keep it so that the children had somewhere familiar to stay when they visited him. Somehow, though, even their visits seemed to be becoming fewer and fewer, and when they did come it was always more to suit Claire than him. And now, of course, the children were growing up and becoming involved with far more activities with their schools and their friends.

The empty house seemed cold and unwelcoming. In the hallway Sam flicked the switch for the central heating but there was a touch of regret about the action because to Sam that always seemed to signify the absolute end of summer. He wasted no time in taking his shower, drying himself then pulling on a polonecked shirt and a pair of grey moleskin trousers.

On his way out of the house he paused to take a bottle of Chardonnay from the rack in the kitchen, and by the time he was back in his car barely half an hour had passed since he had pulled up on the drive.

It was less than a mile to Mill House where Maggie lived with her two children. The house, as its name suggested, was just that—an old converted watermill. The stream ran alongside and the large wooden wheel, dysfunctional these days, nevertheless was still there. The house itself was tucked away in a small valley in the fold of the downs, but even as Sam turned onto the track that led down to it he could see the welcoming amber glow from its windows.

He stopped the car and climbed out, and a chocolate-coloured Labrador ambled forward sniffing the air around her. 'Hello, Galaxy, old girl.' Sam bent and patted her head. 'Where is everyone?'

As if on cue, a golden cocker spaniel appeared round the side of the house and began to bark at the sight of Sam.

'If I thought you were barking a warning instead of a welcome, Rex, I would be really worried.' Sam fondled the spaniel's soft ears and the dog closed his eyes in bliss. A moment later, with the dogs at his heels, Sam rounded the corner of the house and entered a small courtyard. A black studded door off the courtyard was suddenly thrown open and Maggie's daughter, Jessica, appeared in the doorway.

'Sam's here!' she cried. 'Hi, Sam!'

'Hi, Jess.' Sam grinned then as a small boy appeared behind his sister he added, 'Wills, good to see you.'

And suddenly Maggie was there in the doorway of her house; tall and slender in a long purple skirt with a fringed hem and a lavender-coloured cardigan, which she wore as a blouse, the cloud of her dark hair tumbling over her face, the whole effect somehow ethnic and gypsy-like.

'Come in, Sam,' she said in her low, faintly husky voice, and he stepped across the threshold to warmth and aromatic odours from the kitchen, and soft lights and the musky smell of scented candles burning in the room beyond.

'I like Sam.' William picked up the cereal packet and began to pour.

'We all do, dummy,' said Jessica as she nibbled a slice of toast.

'I think he should live here,' William went on.

'William!' Maggie turned from the Aga. 'Look what you're doing. You have far too many crispies there!'

'I'm hungry—and they're not crispies, they're honey flakes.'

'All right, honey flakes. But that's quite enough.'

'Sam can't live here,' Jessica continued calmly. 'He has his own house.'

'But it's a big house.'

'He has to have a big house for when Richard and Emma come to stay.'

'Does Claire come to stay with them?' asked William solemnly.

'Of course not,' replied Jessica scornfully. 'They're divorced, aren't they, Mum?'

'What's that, dear?' Maggie was opening her mail and was already preoccupied.

'Sam and Claire,' Jessica said.

'Sam and Claire.' Maggie frowned. 'Sam and Claire are divorced.'

'Yes, I *know*. That's what I was saying!' Jessica gave an exasperated sigh.

'I still don't see why Sam couldn't live here,' grumbled William as he shovelled spoonfuls of cereal into his mouth. 'Richard and Emma could stay, too, when they wanted to. They could share our rooms.'

'Honestly! You're so stupid at times.' Jessica got up from the table.

'Jessica…' said Maggie warningly.

'Well, he is. I'm sorry but he just is.' She turned and flounced out of the room, passing Ingrid, their nanny-cum-housekeeper, in the doorway.

'I've stripped the beds,' said Ingrid, frowning after Jessica then shrugging and looping her long fair hair back behind one ear.

'Thank you, Ingrid.' Maggie looked up from her bank statements, which seemed to grow more daunting with every month that passed. 'Oh, Ingrid,' she said quickly, 'you'll find some fresh produce in a box in the utility room. There are eggs, apples, tomatoes and a few late runner beans.'

'From Mr North?' asked Ingrid.

Maggie nodded. 'Yes. He and Daisy are so kind.'

'They could, though, couldn't they, Mum?' William finished his breakfast and pushed the bowl away.

'Who could what?' asked Maggie vaguely as she gathered up the bank statements.

'Sam could live here with us,' William said patiently, 'and Richard and Emma could come to stay whenever they wanted to.'

Maggie stared at her son in astonishment. 'Whatever gave you that idea, William?'

'I thought it was a good idea,' muttered William stubbornly. 'I haven't got anyone to play football with now. Jessica won't play…and, well, Dad can't come back, can he?' His eyes suddenly looked suspiciously bright.

'Oh, darling.' Maggie, suddenly realising what her small son's reasoning was about, stood up, moved swiftly round the table and gave him a hug, at the same time dropping a kiss onto the top of his tousled head. 'No,' she whispered into his hair, 'Dad can't come back.'

'Well, then…'

'But neither can Sam come and live here. He has his own home,' she explained.

'Perhaps he could sell it,' said William hopefully. 'Then he could live here with us like Daddy did.'

'But Daddy was my husband—that was different.'

'Couldn't you and Sam get married?' William persisted.

'It doesn't work like that, darling,' said Maggie gently. 'You have to be in love with someone before you marry them.'

'Don't you love Sam?' William sounded quite accusing now.

'Well, he's a very dear friend…'

'Well, then.' William looked faintly exasperated. 'Just get married—I know.' His face flushed with sudden triumph. 'Richard and Emma could come and live here as well!'

'Richard and Emma live with Claire.'

'I know, but—' William opened his mouth to argue his point further.

'No, William.' Maggie spoke gently but firmly in the tone that both her children knew meant that the matter was closed. Looking up at the kitchen clock, she said, 'Heavens, is that the time? I shall be late. I must fly. Ingrid, don't forget Jessica has a dental appointment after school.'

'And I've got football practice,' said William.

'I know. I know,' said Ingrid. 'And I'll collect your suit from the cleaners, Maggie, and take Galaxy to the vet for her check-up.'

'Bless you, Ingrid,' said Maggie with a sigh. 'What would I do without you?'

Half an hour later she was in her car driving towards Millbury, leaving Ingrid to cope with the school run.

She might have missed the autumnal feeling the previous morning, but there was no doubt whatsoever today that the seasons were on the change. The early morning sun struggled to penetrate the thin blanket of mist that hung, wraith-like, throughout the valley. Crystal dewdrops sparkled on every blade of grass while cobwebs, like so many lace doilies, hung between the gateposts and festooned hedgerows already laden with fruit, berries and old man's beard. Percy North would, no doubt, say this signified a hard winter to come, but Maggie loved the feel of autumn and her spirits lifted as she drove.

She had enjoyed supper with Sam the previous evening. The children had joined them for the meal but afterwards they had disappeared to their rooms, William to bed and Jessica to complete her homework. And she and Sam had spread themselves out amongst the many comfortable cushions strewn across her sofas and relaxed as they'd drunk endless cups of coffee, listened to music and talked. Maggie had kicked off her shoes, tucked her legs up beneath her and curled up in a corner of one sofa while Sam had sat on the other, his long legs stretched out before him.

It had been an utterly comfortable and easy evening, one of many really, and it wasn't difficult to understand why William had said what he had at breakfast. Maggie smiled then felt a tug at her heartstrings as she recalled the reasoning behind William's logic. He still missed his father terribly, she knew that, and he loved having a man around.

And who better than someone like Sam, whom he'd known from babyhood? Indeed, Sam was his godfather, just as she was godmother to Sam's daughter Emma. In fact, it had been David who had first brought Sam to the Isle of Wight all those years ago when they'd been at medical school. Then Sam had met Claire and they'd married.

She and David had also married, but whereas there had been an element of surprise over Sam's and Claire's wedding, hers and David's had been entirely predictable. They had been childhood sweethearts, both from old Isle of Wight families, hers with a farming background and

David's with a medical tradition. They had attended the same schools but had been accepted for different universities. Against all the pressures of student life their romance had survived and they had carried out their training in various mainland hospitals before returning to the Island. Everyone had expected them to marry and no one had been surprised when they'd bought Mill House and David had settled down to the life of a country GP.

The surprise over Sam marrying Claire had come about because everyone had assumed that Claire would marry Luke Tyler, the son of a wealthy local builder whom she had dated since high-school days.

Maybe it would have been better if she'd done that in the first place, thought Maggie grimly. It might have caused considerably less anguish. As it was, it had taken Claire a few years and two children to realise that she had loved Luke Tyler all along. By this time David and Sam, together with Leonard Ward, had established the medical centre and Sam had settled down to Island life.

As Maggie climbed out of her car in the medical centre car park, Sam drove in and parked alongside her.

'Morning Maggie.' He smiled through the open window. 'Thanks for supper last night. It was great.'

'Good to have you, Sam.' She retrieved her case from the back of her car and slammed the door. They fell into step. 'I enjoyed it as well,' she added.

'It's getting to be a habit,' he replied. 'You must let me do supper one night.'

'Don't worry about it.' Maggie shrugged. 'It's easier for you to come to me, what with the children and everything.'

'Maybe, but even so I'd like to do something, some time. If it goes on like this, people will think I'm living at Mill House.'

'Funny you should say that.' Maggie laughed, and as Sam raised his eyebrows she went on, 'William said this morning that he can't see why you don't come and live with us. Richard and Emma could come, too, he said, whenever they like or, better still, they could live with us as well!'

'Children are funny, aren't they?' he said, and then casually he added, 'On the other hand, maybe Wills has a point.'

'What do you mean?' Maggie's gaze met his and momentarily there was an expression in Sam's dark eyes that she'd never seen before.

'Well, I suppose to a child it would seem the logical thing to do,' he replied. 'I no longer have a wife and you are on your own. We spend a lot of time together anyway—I guess William just thought it would simplify things all round if we lived in the same house.'

'He likes you being around,' said Maggie quickly. For one moment there she'd imagined Sam was suggesting they should get married. By this time they had reached the door. Sam held it open and stood back for her to precede him. 'He still misses David terribly,' she went on.

Sam nodded. 'I'm sure he does. Poor little chap. I told him I'd go and watch his next football match.'

'He'll like that. Thanks, Sam.' Maggie threw him a grateful glance.

'No problem. I shall enjoy it.' They walked towards Reception then Sam paused. 'Talking of children, Richard and Emma are coming next weekend. I wondered if perhaps we could all do something together.'

'Of course—love to.' Maggie nodded. 'But don't you want to spend time alone with them?'

'I'm always afraid they'll be bored,' he admitted—a trifle sheepishly, she thought.

'I'm sure that's not the case,' Maggie reassured him. 'They love coming to you. I know they do. But we can work something out, I'm sure.' They walked into Reception and were immediately pounced upon, Sam by Jackie to discuss a request for a house visit and Maggie by Katie who wanted her to sign a repeat prescription.

Maggie eventually climbed the stairs to her consulting room, dumped her case on her desk, scanned a couple of letters in her morning's post and was just taking off her jacket when Fiona appeared in the open doorway. She looked brisk and efficient in a dark suit and crisp white blouse.

'Fiona, come in.'

'Sorry. Is this a bad time? I only wanted a quick word.'

'It's OK.' Maggie gave a rueful smile. 'If you wait for a good time, you may wait for ever. How's it going?' she added.

'All right, I think.' Fiona nodded. 'Gradually getting everything sorted out. Moira's been a tremendous help.'

'So how can I help?'

'Well, it's a personal thing really. I wondered if I could register with you.'

'Officially, it's Sam's list that's open at the moment.'

'Yes, I know,' Fiona replied, 'but I prefer a female doctor.'

'Very well.' Maggie nodded. 'I'll mention it to Sam but there won't be a problem. Fill in the necessary forms then pop along and see me some time, either before or after surgery—unless, of course, there's anything you need right away…'

'Oh, no, nothing like that,' Fiona replied hastily. 'I'm quite healthy at the moment.'

'I'm glad to hear it.' Maggie laughed. 'That's not something I hear very often in this room.'

'I can imagine. Anyway, I'll leave you to it—I need to go and do battle with the staff rosters.'

'Rather you than me.' Maggie pulled a face.

Fiona paused one hand on the door handle. 'Shall I tell the girls you're ready for your first patient?'

'No, ask them to give me five minutes,' Maggie replied. As the door closed behind Fiona she sat down at her desk and began to leaf through the rest of the morning's mail. It was always a problem if patients began arriving before she'd had the chance to catch up on test or X-ray results.

One result in particular caught her eye. It was the result of blood tests for Ingrid's mother, Ellen Peters, which Maggie herself had requested. A further check on that morning's surgery list revealed that Ellen had an appointment. The first person on the list, however, was a middle-aged woman by the name of Nadine Harrington, and when Maggie pressed the buzzer she came into the room accompanied by her husband, Bob. Maggie noticed that she looked pale and drawn and that her glance kept darting around the room as if she feared someone else might be watching or listening.

'Hello, Nadine, Bob. Come in, please, and sit down.' Maggie indicated the two chairs alongside her desk, and when they were both seated she said, 'Now, how may I help you?'

'It's her depression, Doctor,' said Bob gloomily. 'And the agoraphobia. It's worse than ever. She won't go anywhere. I had the devil of a job getting her to come here to see you this morning.'

'But you were doing so well the last time I saw you.' Maggie frowned. 'What's happened to change things, Nadine?'

'She had an upset with a neighbour,' Bob explained. 'This brought on a couple of panic attacks—and she wasn't sleeping so we saw Dr Neville and he changed her tablets—'

'You saw Dr Neville?' Maggie frowned. 'When was that?'

'Two or three weeks ago. You were off duty. Anyway, I don't think these new tablets are doing her any good.'

'Let's see.' Maggie clicked onto Nadine's medication chart on the computer. The entry was there. Sam had indeed seen Nadine Harrington and had given her extra medication.

'I tell you, Dr Hudson, she's been terrible lately,' said Bob.

'Tell me, Nadine.' Maggie leaned forward. 'In what way are you worse?'

Tears sprang to Nadine's eyes and she shook her head.

'It's the depression, Doctor,' Bob explained. 'There are some mornings she can't even get out of bed, and when she does she just sits and cries.'

'What about eating? What's her appetite like?' It was obvious that Maggie wasn't going to get any answers from Nadine so she addressed her questions to her husband.

'She eats like a bird,' he replied.

'And sleeping?'

'She seems to go off all right, and then she's awake again about two o'clock. She sometimes doesn't go off at all after that.'

Maggie turned her head and, looking at Nadine, saw the despair in her eyes. 'I'm going to prescribe you some different tablets, Nadine,' she replied. 'They should help you to sleep, but you must take them as well as your usual antidepressants.' She paused. 'You are still taking your antidepressants, aren't you?'

It was Bob who answered. 'Oh, no, Dr Hudson, we stopped those when Dr Neville gave her the others.'

'I'm sure what Dr Neville intended,' said Maggie patiently, 'was that Nadine should take the tablets he prescribed alongside her existing medication.'

'That wasn't what he said,' said Bob doggedly.

'Well, make sure she goes back on them straight away. I've added a further supply to the prescription but I want to see Nadine again in two weeks' time so perhaps you could make an appointment on the way out.'

'All right, Dr Hudson. Thank you.' The Harringtons stood up and left the consulting room with Nadine not having uttered a single word.

With a sigh Maggie pressed the buzzer for her next patient. Ellen Peters was the last patient on her morning surgery list. She was a charming woman but, through Ingrid, Maggie knew her to be tough and fiercely independent. Ellen was actually registered with Sam but she'd previously consulted Maggie with severe pain in her neck and shoulders when Sam had been on holiday. Her appetite had been poor and she'd suffered some weight loss and extreme fatigue so Maggie had arranged for her to have a series of blood tests. She had asked Ellen to attend her surgery for the results.

'How have you been, Ellen?' she asked as the woman came slowly into the room and carefully sat down.

'Not too good,' Ellen replied. 'The painkillers you gave me hardly seemed to touch it, Dr Hudson. Honestly, I'm so stiff, especially first thing in the morning, that I can barely move.'

'Well, Ellen, I think we may be looking at a possible reason for that,' Maggie replied. 'The blood tests that I sent you for show that you may have a condition called polymyalgia. I'll arrange for you to see a specialist for complete confirmation of this, and he may well want you to have a muscle biopsy in due course. In the meantime, I would like to put you on a course of steroids.'

'Oh, dear.' Ellen looked agitated. 'I don't like the sound of that. You hear such dreadful things about steroids.'

'You'll obtain tremendous relief in a very short space of time,' Maggie said patiently. 'It may well be that after a while we can reduce the dose, but that will be for the specialist and Dr Neville to decide. I'll also be referring you to an eye specialist.'

'An eye specialist?' Ellen looked up quickly in surprise then winced with pain at the sudden movement. 'Whatever for?'

'It's just a precautionary measure,' Maggie explained gently. 'In some cases with this condition there can be problems with eyesight so we need to make sure. Your blood test also showed that your haemoglobin is low, which means you're anaemic, so along with the steroids I'll prescribe an iron supplement. Now, Ellen, is there anything you want to ask me?'

'I…' Ellen looked bewildered. 'Will it get better?' she asked at last.

'Like I say, the steroids should bring about a rapid improvement,' Maggie turned to the computer. 'My advice to you, Ellen, is to get started on them as soon as possible. You should soon get your appointment to see the specialist. But if you have any worries in the meantime, don't hesitate to get back to us.'

'All right, Dr Hudson…thank you.' A rather subdued Ellen Peters left Maggie's room. Maggie watched her go then with a sigh she stretched before pressing the intercom button.

'Yes, Dr Hudson?' a voice replied.

'Katie. Is there anyone else for me?'

'One moment, Doctor, I'll just check. No, that was the last.'

'Very well. Thank you. Oh, Katie, has Dr Neville finished yet?'

'Yes, I think he's in the staffroom.'

'Thanks, Katie. I'll catch him there.'

She wanted to see Sam. She wanted to ask him if he'd intended Nadine Harrington to stop her antidepressants—which she was sure he hadn't—and she wanted to tell him about Ellen Peters who, after all, was his patient. But apart from that she wanted to see him for another reason.

Ever since early that morning and that moment in the car park, something at the back of Maggie's mind had been niggling her. She wasn't even sure she knew what it was, that she could even give it form or substance, but it had been something to do with the expression in Sam's eyes when he'd suggested that maybe Wills had a point about them living together. He had been joking, she was sure of that—well, ninety-nine per cent sure—but that expression still bugged her because it was one that she didn't understand, and only yesterday she'd been kidding herself that she knew everything there was to know about Sam and that she could read him like a book.

CHAPTER THREE

'SAM, Ellen Peters has just been to see me.'

'Ellen Peters? Why did she come to you?' Sam poured two coffees from the machine on the counter in the staff-room and handed one to Maggie.

'I saw her when you were on holiday,' Maggie replied. 'She presented with severe shoulder and neck pain. I gave her painkillers and sent her for blood tests. I asked her to come back to see me. The tests came back this morning and it seems we're looking at polymyalgia.'

'Really?' Sam had been about to take a mouthful of coffee but he paused and looked at her, the mug poised halfway to his mouth. 'What have you done?'

'I've referred her to John Temple and started her on a course of steroids. I'll also be writing to the eye clinic.'

'Thanks, Maggie.' Sam nodded. 'How did Ellen take it?' he asked after a moment.

'I don't think she liked the idea of steroids,' Maggie replied. 'But on the other hand, I think her pain is so severe…' She trailed off without finishing the sentence.

'I'll keep an eye on her. It never fails to amaze me how you can treat a patient for years for the usual minor ailments, but when something serious crops up you're away and it's left to a partner to deal with it.'

'That's so often the case,' Maggie agreed. She paused and glanced at Sam. He was facing her as if waiting for her to say something else. There was no sign now of that expression that had been in his eyes earlier and Maggie found herself wondering if she'd imagined it. She took a deep breath. 'Speaking of seeing each other's patients,' she went on, 'Nadine Harrington came to see me today.'

'Nadine Harrington...' Sam frowned. 'Oh, yes, I know. I saw her a little while ago. Remind me...what was it?'

'She has a long history of agoraphobia, panic attacks and depression.' Maggie sat down and, curling her hands around her mug, sipped the coffee.

'Ah, yes, that's right.' Sam nodded. 'I remember now. There had been some dispute with her neighbours over a hedge or something—she'd suffered several panic attacks, was very agitated and she was having difficulty sleeping. I prescribed a mild tranquilliser.' He threw Maggie a side-long glance. 'Was there a problem with that?'

'No, not really.' She shrugged. 'The problem arose from discontinuing her antidepressants.'

'Who told her to do that?' Sam stared at her.

'She said you did, or rather her husband said that you did. Nadine herself actually said nothing.'

'But I didn't tell her to discontinue her medication.' Sam looked faintly exasperated. 'I told her to take the new tablets in addition to the others.'

'That's what I thought.' Maggie nodded.

'I thought her husband had understood my instructions but maybe he was more agitated about her than I thought. Obviously I didn't make myself plain. Sorry, Maggie.'

'It's OK. I always feel that's the problem with seeing each other's patients—we don't know them as well as our own.'

'What would you have done with the Harringtons in that situation?' asked Sam curiously after a moment.

'Repeated my instructions several times to make sure they understood, or even written it down and given it to Bob Harrington,' Maggie replied. 'He's pretty good as a rule over Nadine's medication but unfortunately he does sometimes get muddled. Anyway, don't worry about it. I've sorted them out now.' She took another mouthful of coffee. 'Have you thought anymore about the weekend?' she asked after a moment.

Sam had started signing repeat prescriptions but he looked up. 'Well, if it's fine I thought perhaps a long walk with the dogs, maybe a picnic, then all back to my place for a spaghetti Bolognese. How does that sound?'

'Sounds OK to me.' Maggie swallowed as she was forced to battle with a sudden rush of memories.

'I doubt the kids will all agree.' Sam laughed. 'There's bound to be one of them or maybe even two who'll want to do something totally different. But what the hell—we'd never get it so right as to please all of them, so we just have to go for it.'

'That's true.' Maggie stared into the bottom of her mug for a moment then, draining it, she jumped to her feet. 'This won't do,' she said. 'I've house calls to make.' With her head down she hurried from the staffroom, only too aware that Sam was watching her from his chair with a slightly puzzled expression on his face. It wasn't that she didn't want to go out with him and his children at the weekend—far from it, it was the sort of thing that was good for them all—but the talk of walks and picnics had brought back such vivid images of when David had been alive that momentarily it had overwhelmed her. This was how it happened. She would be perfectly all right one minute, talking quite rationally about everyday things, then it would all wash over her again. Anything could trigger it—talk of the past, a snatch of music or a particular smell, like newly mown grass or barbecue smoke on a summer's evening. It was getting less, she had to admit that, but when it did happen it threw her completely.

Grabbing the notes for her house calls, her jacket and

her car keys, she hurried down the stairs and out of the building through the back door, thus avoiding the probability of being waylaid in Reception either by staff or patients.

She carried out both house visits, one to a new mother and baby who lived in the old coastguard cottages on the far side of Millbury and the other in one of the outlying villages to an elderly lady who was bedridden with severe osteoporosis and who had developed an acute case of pleurisy.

It was while she was driving back towards Millbury that she passed a house with a table outside bearing a couple of buckets filled with dahlias and chrysanthemums. On a sudden impulse she stopped and bought a bunch of each, leaving the money in the pot provided.

It was only a five-minute drive from there to the church of St Peter and St Paul where she and David had married, where the children had been christened and where David's funeral had been held.

Parking the car in the lane beside the ivy-covered churchyard wall, Maggie gathered up the flowers and made her way through the lych-gate and round the side of the church. Sunlight and shadow played upon the flagstone path that divided the older lichen-encrusted graves and led to a cleared area at the back of the church. Here the headstones were newer—black granite or mottled brown stone.

David's grave was at the end of a row beside a yew tree, peaceful in a patch of sunlight. A wilting bunch of white daisies were still in the pot beneath the black headstone where Jessica had placed them on their last visit on the anniversary of David's birthday. The gold lettering on the shiny black stone stated that David Spencer Hudson, beloved husband, son and father, had died aged thirty-

seven years together with the date. A further line added
that he would live on for ever in the hearts of those who
loved him.

Maggie disposed of the dying flowers, filled the pot
with fresh water from a tap against the church wall then,
sinking to her knees on the grass beside the grave, began
to sort out the purple dahlias and golden chrysanthemums.

There was hardly a sound in the churchyard, just the
hum of a solitary bee and the occasional sound of a car
as it passed by on the road outside. David's funeral had
taken place on a day such as this when the sun had been
warm on their shoulders and the gold and russet of the
trees around the church had been in strong contrast to the
deep blue of the sky. Not that Maggie remembered much
about that day for she seemed to have gone through the
entire proceedings on autopilot. Sam had taken over from
the moment David had died and had organised everything.
It didn't seem possible that over a year had passed since
then and yet, at other times, it had felt like the longest
year of her life.

In her heart she felt as if it had actually been two years
since she'd lost David for in that last year of his life, when
he'd battled against the cancer that had finally claimed
him, he'd been but a pale shadow of the man she'd married and each day she'd felt him slipping a little further
away from her. She'd thought she'd been prepared for his
death—after all, as a doctor she'd seen suffering and death
often enough—but it had come as a terrible shock. She'd
had to be strong for the children and to a certain extent
working in the practice had helped enormously but, if she
was really honest, it had been Sam who had pulled her
through. Sam, who had been there whenever she'd needed
someone, Sam who had allowed her to rant and rave about
the injustice of it all, to vent her anger—such terrible an-

ger that she wondered where it had come from—and Sam who had allowed her to grieve. And it had been Sam who had helped with her workload or sorted out the children whenever it had all threatened to become too much for her.

Maggie knew that now, at last, she was coming through it, knew that the time was coming when she would need to take stock, to pick up the pieces of her life and to move on. As she put the last flower in the pot she sat back on her heels to admire the arrangement. David would have approved she felt sure—chrysanthemums had been his favourite flowers. Sturdy and dependable was how he'd described them—just like him really, she thought. She stood up and through a sudden mist of tears she looked down at David's final resting place then she moved away and with one last backward glance at the quiet grave with its bright splash of colour she made her way back up the sun-dappled path to the lych-gate.

'Well, you certainly seem to be healthy.' Maggie straightened up and draped her stethoscope round her neck. 'Weight, pulse and blood pressure are all normal. Is there anything you think I need to know about before your medical records arrive from your last GP?' It was the following morning and Fiona had come to Maggie's consulting room for her check-up before surgery started. 'Any allergies or anything?' Maggie added.

'I get hay fever,' Fiona admitted. 'But I'm all right at this time of year.'

'Any asthma?'

'As a child, yes, slightly, but not now. I also occasionally suffer from migraine but I have to admit that was when I was taking the Pill.'

Maggie looked up, her pen poised. 'You no longer take it?'

Fiona shook her head. 'No, I was in a relationship but it ended a year or so ago. I didn't see any point in taking unnecessary medication.'

'Probably very wise,' Maggie agreed. 'So there's no one in your life at the moment?'

Fiona shook her head. 'No. I'm free, and loving every minute of it.' She paused. 'That's not to say that if the right man came along... Mind you, at the moment I'm still trying to work out all the various liaisons amongst the staff.'

'I warned you it was all pretty convoluted, didn't I?' said Maggie with a laugh.

'I think I've got most of it sussed now. I've had to be careful, though. It's so easy to put one's foot in it if you don't know who's with who or, more to the point, who used to be with who.'

'Best to ask if you're not sure.'

'Yes.' Fiona nodded then after a moment she began, 'Actually, now you come to mention it...'

Maggie had been entering notes on the computer, but she looked up again.

'There was just one thing...'

'What's that?'

Fiona hesitated as if still unsure of what she was about to say. 'You and Dr Neville...' she began at last.

'What about me and Dr Neville?' asked Maggie with a frown.

'Oh, nothing,' said Fiona hastily. 'It's nothing really.'

'No, go on, please.' Maggie sat back in her chair. 'I'm interested.'

'Well, it's just that I wondered... You seem...you seem

so...'. Fiona floundered slightly. 'Are you an item?' she said at last, coming to the point.

'Heavens, no!' Maggie exclaimed.

'Sorry. I've been jumping to conclusions. I know you lost your husband...but you and Dr Neville you seem so—'

'That's because we're such good friends,' Maggie replied quietly. 'But that's all we are,' she added.

'I see.' Fiona nodded. 'I'm sorry. But it wasn't just me who thought so...the others also seem to be under the same impression.'

'In that case, you'll be able to put them right,' said Maggie with a short laugh.

'I will.' Fiona smiled. 'Mind you, you can hardly blame them. There's always speculation of some kind, even though it usually involves Jon. But, no, you can't blame them, and you have to admit, he *is* gorgeous.'

'Yes, he is,' Maggie agreed with a smile. 'But there's no need to tell him because Jon's trouble is that he already knows it.'

'Oh, I wasn't talking about Jon,' said Fiona, 'although I'll grant you he's pretty gorgeous, too. No, I was referring to Dr Neville.'

'Oh,' said Maggie. Just for a moment she was lost for words.

'I can't understand how he's remained single as long as he has,' Fiona went on. 'I guess the women on the Isle of Wight must have trouble with their eyesight.'

'Maybe it's something to do with Sam himself...'

'You mean, once bitten twice shy?' Fiona raised her eyebrows. 'In my experience that in itself could present something of a challenge.'

'Yes, well...I dare say.'

Maggie was in a thoughtful mood as Fiona left the

room. It was interesting how others perceived a situation, and hearing Fiona describe Sam as gorgeous had stirred some emotion within her. She should have guessed there would be speculation amongst the staff about Sam and herself. After all, they did spend a lot of time in each other's company. But he was her friend. Her best friend in the entire world. They'd been friends for a very long time. When it had been the four of them they'd spent quite a bit of time together, she and David and Sam and Claire, and after the children had been born they'd shared outings, parties and barbecues. It was inevitable, really, in view of all that had happened that she and Sam should still seek each other's company.

Maybe they were both clinging to the past—to how it had once been—as if by being together they could somehow turn the clock back to a time when Claire had still loved Sam and David had been alive. And if they were still clinging to the past, probably by now they should have both moved on—especially if people were putting their own interpretations on the situation.

There was no romance between herself and Sam and there never had been. As far as Maggie was concerned, romance should hold an element of mystery—it was the one aspect in her romance with David that she would have changed if she could, the fact that they'd known each other so well—and with Sam they'd already been through so much together, sharing each other's grief and pain, it was as if all their emotions had been stripped bare, with nothing left to discover.

Maybe it was time to mention to Sam that perhaps they should both try and move on…that people were talking. Maggie sighed. Perhaps she would say something at the weekend if the opportunity arose. On the other hand, did it matter? If they were comfortable in each other's company purely as friends, did it really matter what anyone else thought?

She was about to press her buzzer for her first patient of the morning when her intercom suddenly sounded. She leaned over the desk and flicked the switch.

'Dr Hudson?'

'Yes, Jackie?'

'Can you take a visit?'

'Who is it?'

'Alison Scott. She's bleeding again.'

'Remind me. How far is she now?'

'Eleven weeks. I've told her to rest quietly in bed with her legs elevated.'

'Very well, Jackie, tell her I'll be with her shortly. Is there someone with her?'

'Yes, her husband Rory's there. He made the call.'

'OK. Thanks.'

Maggie left the surgery immediately. Alison and Rory lived on a farm just off the coast road. Alison was expecting her first baby but she had a history of miscarriage. Indeed, with this latest pregnancy she'd already suffered one threatened miscarriage at seven weeks. The couple were desperate for a child and Maggie knew they would both be seriously concerned by this latest setback.

The farm was large and until fairly recently had been a fully working farm which had employed many people but, like so many others, with changing trends in farming Rory had been forced to sell his dairy herd and put his acres of land to producing rape seed and linseed oil. In another attempt to diversify, the Scotts had turned their old stone farmhouse into a bed and breakfast establishment, with Rory swapping his farming overalls for a chef's apron and Alison selling preserves and dried flowers from trestle tables in the old barn,

Times had been difficult for the couple—Maggie knew that just as she knew that they'd refused to be beaten, whether in their efforts to keep their farm or in their attempts to start a family.

There were a couple of cars parked in the yard alongside the battered Land Rover that Rory drove and Alison's Metro. As Maggie climbed out of her own car, a middle-aged couple came out of the farmhouse laden with luggage.

'Good morning.' The man looked across at Maggie and nodded. 'If you're coming here to stay, you're in for a treat, I can tell you.'

'We had the works for breakfast,' said his wife. 'Grapefruit, cereal, egg, bacon, sausages, mushrooms, tomatoes…'

'And fried bread,' added her husband.

'Yes, and fried bread,' the woman agreed. 'Then we finished up with toast and marmalade.'

Maggie smiled. 'No, I haven't come to stay. But I almost wish I were. You're making me feel quite hungry.' She looked up as Rory suddenly appeared in the doorway.

'Hello, Rory,' she said.

'Hello, Doctor.'

The man had been loading bags into the boot of his car but he turned round smartly. 'Doctor?' he said in surprise.

'Yes,' Maggie replied pleasantly. 'Enjoy the rest of your holiday, but watch your cholesterol level,' she added with a smile as she followed Rory indoors.

'Good job you weren't here before they ate their breakfast,' Rory said over his shoulder as he led the way upstairs.

'Quite,' Maggie replied dryly. 'How's Alison?' she added.

'Resting.' Rory led the way along a narrow passage to the far end where he unlatched a door and pushed it open.

'Alison, love,' he said gently, 'Maggie's here.' He stood back for Maggie to enter the room, and as he did so they heard the faint sound of a bell ringing downstairs. 'That'll be the other guests, wanting to check out,' he muttered.

'You go down, Rory,' said Maggie.

Alison was lying in bed, her feet raised on a couple of pillows. She looked tired and drawn and her eyes were red and puffy as if she'd been crying.

'Hello, Alison.' Maggie came right into the room as Rory clattered off down the stairs and set her case down on a chair.

'Oh, Maggie.' Fresh tears welled up in Alison's eyes. 'It's happening again.'

'Not necessarily.' Maggie perched on the edge of the bed and took hold of Alison's hand. She'd known the Scott family for years and was fond of both Alison and Rory. 'Tell me what happened,' she went on.

'The usual.' Alison dabbed her eyes then blew her nose. 'I had a backache when I got out of bed this morning. I went to the bathroom and I noticed a smear of blood. I got back into bed straight away. Rory told me to rest while he cooked breakfast. The backache eased up but later when I went back to the bathroom I was bleeding. I called Rory and he phoned you immediately. Oh, Maggie, I don't want to lose this baby. I really don't. It's gone longer than the others and I was daring to hope that this time it was for real.'

'And it still could be,' Maggie replied firmly.

'Do I have to go to hospital?'

'Well, I'd like to have a look at you first.' Maggie folded back the bedclothes and gently proceeded to examine Alison's abdomen. When she'd finished she replaced the covers and washed her hands in the hand basin in the corner of the bedroom.

'It's not looking too bad at the moment,' she said at last as she dried her hands on a small hand towel. 'The bleeding is very slight and, provided you rest, I think we may be in with a chance. But I do mean rest, Alison.'

'Oh, I will. I will,' Alison replied fervently.

'No slipping off downstairs to help with the breakfasts or nipping out to the barn to set up your dried flowers.'

'No, absolutely not. We have Mrs Higgs come in to give Rory a hand and, well, the dried flowers will just have to wait.' Alison paused. 'So I won't have to go to hospital?'

'Not for the moment. We'll see how things go. I'm going to give you an injection just to be on the safe side.' Maggie opened her case and took out a packet containing a disposable syringe then took an ampoule from her medication tray. Within minutes she had administered the injection. 'I may want you to go and have an ultrasound at the hospital in a few days' time,' she said as she closed her case, 'but for the time being all that's necessary is complete bed rest. Now, I'll call back again to see you, Alison, but if you're at all worried just ask Rory to phone the centre.'

'Yes, all right, Maggie. And thank you. Thank you so much.'

Maggie went downstairs and made her way through to the kitchen where she found Rory loading the dishwasher and Mrs Higgs, the daily help, collecting together her cleaning materials in readiness to attack the bedrooms. They both looked up anxiously as Alison appeared.

'How is she, poor lamb?' asked Mrs Higgs.

'She's resting quietly,' Maggie said, 'and I've impressed on her that's what she has to do. Complete bed rest, at least for the next few days.' As Mrs Higgs disappeared into the hall Maggie turned to Rory.

'Is the baby safe?' he asked, and she could see the fear in his eyes.

'I hope so,' she replied. 'I've given Alison an injection which should help. But she really does have to rest, Rory. I think she understands that but I'm relying on you to keep an eye on her as well. There must be no nipping downstairs because she's remembered something that needs doing.'

'All right, Maggie, I understand, but I don't think you'll find she'll take any chances. Not this time. We really want this baby, you know.'

'Yes, Rory,' said Maggie. 'I know you do.' Reaching out, she gently touched his arm. 'And we'll do all we can to make sure everything is all right this time.'

Leaving the farm, she drove back to start her morning surgery. When she arrived it was to find chaos, with a packed waiting room, harassed reception staff, crying children and a stream of patients growing more fidgety by the minute.

Squaring her shoulders, Maggie prepared to enter the fray.

CHAPTER FOUR

SAM stood in the centre of his kitchen and looked around. What had he forgotten? He had cola, crisps, fruit yoghurts, fish fingers, chicken nuggets, toffee-flavoured ice cream, pasta and Marmite, probably at least half of which he, as a doctor, should be discouraging. But he saw his children so infrequently that it was irresistible when they did come to stay to stock up with all their favourites.

In the early days when he and Claire had first parted it had seemed that whenever access visits had been arranged he'd been on call and had had to cancel. This had led to Claire becoming less and less co-operative about him seeing the children. But since the practice had joined the Island on-call system life had become much easier, with more doctors to share the workload, resulting in fewer nights or weekends on call. Sam was hoping he could persuade Claire to allow the children to visit him more often. He loved his children dearly and the biggest regret in his life was that he was missing out on a large chunk of their growing up. In fact, if he was really honest, he regretted that more than his parting from Claire.

He had loved her at first, of course he had, and when they'd married he'd truly believed it would last for ever, but it had soon become apparent to him that Claire had still been in love with her old boyfriend, Luke Tyler. Sam had hoped that Claire might get over it in time, especially after their children had been born, and she might have done for by that time Luke Tyler had married and had a family of his own.

It had only been when Luke Tyler's wife had left him, accusing him of still being in love with Claire, that the problems had really started. And it seemed to Sam, on reflection, that from that point there had been no going back.

She'd left him when Richard had been eight years old and Emma five. He'd agreed to a divorce and Claire and Luke Tyler had married a month after the decree absolute had been issued.

It was a very dark time for Sam and all that kept him going was his work and the friendship of David and Maggie. Without them he shuddered to think how he might have ended up. They were there constantly—at work if the workload threatened to overwhelm him, and at home when they would invite him for meals and include him in any family celebrations. He knew he would be grateful to them for the rest of his life for quietly they enabled him to come to terms with his situation. He was just at the point where he felt ready to move on, to get on with his life, when David's illness was diagnosed and it was Sam's turn to extend the hand of friendship.

The sudden sound of a car door slamming brought Sam back to the present with a start. With a final glance round the kitchen, satisfying himself that all was ready, he walked into the hall and was in time to see Emma erupt through the front door.

'Daddy! Hi!' she cried. 'How are you?'

'I'm fine, sweetheart.' Sam hugged her. 'How are you? Let me look at you.' Holding her at arm's length and with his head tilted thoughtfully on one side, he allowed his gaze to roam over his daughter. She wore black trousers, a striped sweater, a black velvet hat and large, clumpy-looking boots. With her dark hair and eyes she resembled him, while Richard, who had followed her into the hall, took after Claire with his fair hair and grey eyes. 'You look fantastic,' said Sam, drawing her close again and dropping a kiss onto her nose. Reaching out one arm, he invited Richard to join them. The boy, his eyes solemn behind his glasses, hung back, but only for a moment, then he, too, was happily reunited with his father in their group hug.

Momentarily Sam was unable to speak, aware of the lump in his throat that always seemed to be there on these occasions, then at last as he released the children and looked up he caught sight of Claire in the doorway. Behind her on the drive he caught a glimpse of her red Saab convertible. With her exquisitely cut hair and her immaculate designer clothes, she squarely met his gaze, and miraculously the lump in his throat dissolved.

'Claire.' He nodded. 'How are you?'

'Busy. I can't stop, Sam. I have people coming to lunch.'

He was about to say that he also had people coming, but he thought better of it. Instead, he said, 'I won't keep you, then. What about tomorrow? Would you like me to bring them back?'

She hesitated only fractionally. 'No, I'll pick them up,' she replied. 'About six o'clock?'

'Yes, that's fine.' Together with the children, he walked out onto the drive and they watched as Claire climbed into her car and started the engine then wound down the window.

'Bye, you two,' she called.

'Bye, Mum.'

With a wave of one slim brown hand she was gone.

'What are we going to do today?' asked Emma as they turned to go back into the house.

'Can I have a go on your computer?' asked Richard.

'Actually, Maggie's coming over with Jessica and William,' said Sam.

'Oh, goody,' cried Emma. 'Will we go out? Will they bring the dogs?'

'Yes to both those questions,' replied Sam with a laugh. 'We thought a long walk, possibly along the top of the downs, then a picnic on the beach.'

'Brill,' cried Emma.

'That suit you, old man?' Sam ruffled Richard's hair.

Richard nodded. 'But can I use the computer until they come?'

'Of course you can.'

'Good.' Richard paused then added, 'I like Maggie. Wills can be a bit of a pain, but I like Maggie.'

It was a long haul up to the top of the downs but the views from the top were well worth the effort. The children ran ahead, chasing the dogs as they foraged in the bracken, while Maggie and Sam paused to catch their breath and admire the view. Below them the curve of the downs fell sharply away and a patchwork of fresh green fields and rich ploughed earth stretched as far as the distant cliffs that bordered the coastal road. Beyond, the perfect cobalt blue of the sea stretched for ever, merging with the sky in a hazy horizon. To their left in the distance they could see the cliffs above Blackgang Chine, while in the other direction the sheer white chalk face towered above Freshwater Bay.

'We're so lucky to live here,' said Maggie, shielding her eyes from the sun.

'True,' Sam agreed. 'I can't imagine why anyone would ever want to leave once they've lived here.'

'You've never had any inclination to go back to the mainland?' Maggie threw him a sidelong glance. He looked casual and relaxed in jeans and a fleece jacket, his hair even more tousled today by the wind.

He shook his head. 'Never. Why should I? I have everything I want right here. My children are here, my work is here and I have the best friends a man could ever wish for.' He paused. 'How about you?'

'Me?' Maggie looked startled. 'What do you mean?'

'Well, have you never had any inclination to move away?'

'Heavens, no! My roots are here and, like you, everyone and everything of any importance in my life is right here.'

'I just wondered if you've ever felt the need for a completely fresh start.'

Maggie shook her head. 'No. If I did that I would somehow feel it would be running away. If I moved away I would be afraid to return because the memories would be too painful. This way I'm learning to live with the memories.'

'I think you've done very well,' said Sam quietly.

'I have my moments still,' Maggie replied.

'I'm sure you do…'

'But I do believe they're getting fewer.'

'What about the children?' Sam turned and looked towards the belt of conifers behind them where the children could be seen rushing around with the two dogs.

'They're much better. Wills sleeps through the night now without any nightmares and Jessica at last has started talking about David. I think the healing process is well under way.'

'I'm glad to hear it.'

Together they turned and began walking the rough chalk pathway along the top of the downs.

'How about you?' Maggie asked after a while.

'What about me?' Sam frowned.

'Well, have you recovered?' They both knew what she meant in spite of the fact that this was a topic that was rarely raised between them.

'Oh, yes, I think so. You have to, you know, otherwise you remain trapped in some ghastly time warp. But I can honestly say that I can look at Claire quite dispassionately now. Take this morning when she brought the children over—it's like she's a stranger now, not someone with whom I once shared my whole life.'

'You'll meet someone else, Sam. I'm sure of that. There has to be someone out there for you—you have so much to give.'

'Maybe.' He shrugged. They walked on in silence for a few minutes. 'Likewise for you,' he said.

'Oh, I doubt it.' Maggie shook her head.

'But you're young…'

'Even so.' She shrugged, snuggling into her jacket as the wind whipped her hair across her face. 'I couldn't imagine it somehow,' she went on after a moment. 'David and I were together almost from the moment we were born. We played together as toddlers, we started school on the same day, we dated through high school. It was always a foregone conclusion that we should marry. It just wouldn't feel right with anyone else.'

'It would be different certainly, in every way,' Sam agreed. 'But that's not to say it wouldn't be right. I also happen to think it would be what David would want. I know he wouldn't have wanted you to live the rest of your life in loneliness.'

'Who says I'm lonely? I have the children.'

'At the moment, yes. But not for ever. They have their own lives to lead and they'll go one day.'

'Are you implying that by then I'll be so old that no one will spare me a second glance?' Maggie pulled a face.

'Of course not,' Sam replied. 'I'm simply saying you have yourself to think about.'

'Well, you're a fine one to talk. How long have you been on your own now? Three years?'

'Four, actually.'

'Well, there you are, then. How many women have you dated in that time?'

'A couple,' he admitted.

'Really?' Maggie was surprised. 'You never said.'

'I didn't think I had to.' He looked faintly embarrassed. 'Besides, they were both utter disasters. Not the women— the relationships.'

They both laughed then stopped as the dogs rushed past them. They turned and waited for the children to catch up. It was the first time they'd talked like this. While they spent much time together, their conversations usually centred on the practice, the children or their mutual acquaintances, never on themselves and the painful times they'd both experienced.

They left the downs, following the narrow chalk path all the way down to the coastal road then across the fields to the clifftop, the dogs racing ahead, and finally down to the beach.

The tide was going out and the newly washed sand was littered with clumps of seaweed and the odd piece of driftwood. Gulls circled overhead, calling noisily as they swooped and dived for insects, while on a distant line of rocks that jutted from the sea a line of cormorants, eyeing the situation, awaited the right moment to dive into the waves.

'We'll pitch up over there under the cliffs,' called Sam, and they all set off across the expanse of hard wet sand towards the shelter of a circle of rocks at the base of the cliffs.

'I'm starving,' grumbled William. 'Isn't it time to eat yet?'

'You're always starving,' said Jessica scornfully.

'Actually, I'm hungry, too,' admitted Richard as he stopped for a moment to wipe the sea spray from his glasses.

'So am I,' said Sam with a laugh. 'It must be all this fresh air. Come on, Wills, I'll race you to the rocks.'

Maggie and the girls watched as Sam, William, Richard and the dogs took off and raced along the beach. It was good to see them for once all happy and enjoying themselves. She turned towards the sea and, throwing her arms wide, took a deep lungful of the bracing sea air. A moment later she felt a tug at her sleeve and, looking down, she found Emma at her side.

'I like it down here,' said Emma with a little sigh. Her cheeks were flushed beneath the brim of her black hat and her eyes sparkled. 'We hardly ever go for walks like this.'

'Why not?' demanded Jessica.

'Mummy doesn't like the beach,' said Emma. 'And Luke is always so busy.'

'But you have your own pony, don't you?' The envy in Jessica's voice was only too obvious and Maggie threw her daughter a quick glance.

Emma nodded. 'Yes.' She sighed. 'I love Mister Snow, but I sometimes wish Mummy and Luke weren't always so busy.'

'What does your mum do?' asked Jessica.

'I don't know really,' Emma admitted. 'But she's always busy going to lunches and things…and shopping. I think she helps Luke as well with his business…' She trailed off uncertainly.

'My mum's always busy, too, aren't you, Mum?' said Jessica.

'Well, yes, I suppose I am,' admitted Maggie.

'But you still go for walks and picnics and things,' said Emma wistfully.

'Come on,' said Maggie. 'Let's go and organise those men and animals, otherwise we'll never eat.'

They all carried small rucksacks on their backs into which Sam and Maggie had packed bread rolls, some filled with cheese and pickle, others with ham and salad and a few with Marmite. There were also crisps, at least three flavours, and chocolate biscuits, and fruit—apples and bananas. Each rucksack also contained a plastic bottle filled with cola or orange juice.

They tucked themselves in amongst the rocks on a small expanse of firm, dry sand in the shelter of the cliffs, which towered above them. There were several friendly squabbles over the food but eventually they all sorted themselves out and fell silent as they began to eat.

Maggie was surprised to find that even she was ravenously hungry. Her appetite hadn't been up to much lately and everyone told her she was too thin, but today, somehow, it seemed different. Maybe it was simply a combination of the exercise she'd had in the long walk over the downs and the bracing sea air, she didn't really know. But whatever it was, her appetite had returned and quite suddenly, sitting on the beach surrounded by her own children and Sam and his children, she felt totally at peace with herself.

She looked round at the others, wondering if they, too, felt as she did. William, predictably, was still eating, a concentrated look of bliss on his face as he chewed a chocolate caramel bar. Emma had finished her lunch and was feeding titbits to Rex, the spaniel, while Galaxy lay panting on the sand. Richard's usually pale complexion was flushed by the sea air as he sat high above them on a rock, staring out to sea, and even Jessica, who just lately had considered this sort of activity to be beneath her, had taken herself off a short distance to sift the shingle for unusual stones or shells.

Sam was lying against his rucksack on a large, flat-topped rock, his hands behind his head. His eyes were closed and he looked utterly relaxed. Maggie found herself studying him and at the same time recalling Fiona's opinion of him. She knew his face almost as well as her own but she doubted whether she'd ever really studied him before.

He wasn't technically handsome in the generally accepted sense of the word. Slightly stocky in build, his dark hair was already starting to show a tinge of grey at the temples, but as she studied him, as if seeing him for the first time, Maggie could see where Fiona's perception came from. His profile was strong, the nose high-bridged and slightly curved, the jaw square and firm, but Maggie knew from everyday experience that it was the warmth of Sam's smile that could melt the most frosty of situations, for his was a smile that was constantly reflected in his eyes. Some people could smile with their mouth only and it would never reach their eyes, but not Sam. If anything, the merriment was in his eyes before his brain called for a response from his mouth.

Almost as if he sensed her scrutiny, he opened one eye and turned his head towards her. On finding her watching him, he opened the other eye and frowned. Removing his hands from behind his head, he propped himself up on one elbow.

'Maggie?' he said softly. 'What's wrong?'

'Nothing.' She shook her head. 'Nothing's wrong.'

'You were staring at me.'

'Sorry. Was I?'

'Yes, as if you hadn't seen me before.'

She gave a short laugh. 'I was just thinking, if asked, how difficult it would be to describe someone you know very well.'

'That's probably very true,' he agreed. After a pause, he said, 'So how would you describe me if you were asked?'

'Let me see.' Putting her head on one side, she surveyed him critically. 'Well, I'm sorry, Sam, but I would have to say you were of stocky build...'

With a muttered exclamation Sam scrambled to his feet. As Maggie moved smartly to get out of his way, over her shoulder she added wickedly, 'And that there are definite signs of greying in your hair...'

'That does it.' He lunged towards her and with a shriek, and to the amusement of the children, she darted off across the sand with Sam in pursuit.

As the wind tugged at her hair and the salt air stung her cheeks, quite suddenly she felt like a teenager again.

Sam finally cornered her amongst a cluster of rocks. Gasping and laughing, she held him at bay.

'Do you take it back?' he demanded as she turned and scrambled up onto the rocks.

Looking wildly around, she realised she was trapped.

'Well, do you?' Sam demanded.

'I do,' she gasped. 'I do.'

'In that case, you'd better come down.' He stood there, arms akimbo, looking up at her as she gazed down at him.

A sudden shout from along the beach caused them both to look up.

'Are we going now?' Jessica had followed them and,

obviously bored by the childish antics of her elders, was watching them with her arms folded.

'Going?' Sam turned to her. 'Going?' he repeated. 'Of course we're not going. We haven't had our game of rounders yet.'

'How can we play rounders?' demanded Jessica disdainfully. 'We haven't got a bat or a ball.'

'What's this, then?' Sam put his hand into his pocket and pulled out a tennis ball. 'And I saw a rather good piece of driftwood over there, which will make an excellent bat.'

'How will we work out the teams?' asked Jessica. She was beginning to sound interested now.

'I suggest boys against the girls,' Sam replied.

'OK.' Jessica nodded. 'You're on. Come on, Mum. Get down from there. We have to show the boys how to play rounders.' She turned and strolled unhurriedly back along the beach.

'Sam.'

He had turned to follow Jessica but he stopped as Maggie called him. 'Yes?' he said innocently.

'I can't get down.'

'Really?' He raised his eyebrows but the amusement was right there in his dark eyes.

'Will you help me? Please?' she added when he simply remained standing there, watching her.

With a chuckle he moved forward, rested one foot against the base of the rocks to steady himself then reached out his hand. 'Come on,' he said. 'Hold onto me, then jump.'

She took hold of his hand. It was warm and strong and she felt safe, knowing that, whatever happened, even if she fell, he would catch her. She jumped and as she landed on the sand would have lost her balance but Sam's arms went around her and steadied her.

'Thanks, Sam.'

For a moment she leaned against him. He felt solid and reassuring and through the fabric of his sweater she could hear the beating of his heart. It was a long time since she'd felt a man's arms around her. It felt good, stirring feelings and emotions which had lain dormant, it seemed, for a lifetime. Briefly she was content to remain there, safe and secure, with no desire or inclination to move. Then the moment passed and there could be no further justification for remaining where she was. She attempted to draw away from him but his arms tightened and she was unable to move.

He held her away from him and looked into her eyes. 'Maggie…' he whispered, and it was then that she realised that expression was back in his eyes—the one she had seen there before and been at a loss to explain. It had bewildered her then and it bewildered her now, but this time it was the stirring of her senses that was the main cause of her bewilderment—a quickening of her pulse together with an increase to her heartbeat.

'Sam, no.' She had to break the moment. 'The children…' She glanced along the beach.

His sigh was barely audible but he released her immediately and together they walked back to the children. Neither of them said a word but it was obvious they were both only too aware of what had just occurred between them.

Sam's advance had startled Maggie, coming as it had right out of the blue. Never before had there been the slightest indication that he wanted their relationship to move into a new arena, and as the game of rounders got under way Maggie found herself wondering if what had just happened would change things in some way. She valued Sam's friendship above most other things in her life, and couldn't bear the thought of losing it. On the other hand, as she'd told Fiona and had just made plain to Sam himself, friendship was all there was between them.

The game became fast and furious, with even the usually cool Jessica darting about over the wet sand, her long fair hair streaming behind her. The shouts of the children mingled with the cries of the sea birds, and they played on until the shadows began to lengthen and the girls were reluctantly forced to accept defeat at the hands of the boys.

'We'll beat you next time,' gasped Emma as she flung herself down onto the sand to recover. 'Won't we, Maggie?'

'We will indeed,' Maggie agreed vehemently.

'Time for home, I think,' said Sam.

'You did say we were having spaghetti, didn't you?' asked William anxiously.

'Absolutely, old son. Come on, everyone, rucksacks on. It's time we were heading for home. It's getting chilly. Put your jacket on, Richard.'

'But I'm hot,' protested Richard.

'That's why you need to put your jacket on as you cool down,' said Sam. He turned. 'All right, Maggie?' His eyes met hers.

'Yes, fine, thanks.' She looked away. 'We're right behind you, Sam.'

In single file, tired but happy, the little band made its way up the steep cliff path, the dogs ambling wearily behind. The tide was on the turn and a keen breeze rippled the waves and blew little flurries of sand against the very rocks in whose shelter they had earlier eaten their picnic. Maggie paused and looked back. The beach looked quite desolate now, almost entirely in shadow with the sun sinking fast behind the cliffs and the sky turning to opalescent grey. She shivered, pulling her jacket around her and fastening the zip before continuing on up the path to the road.

CHAPTER FIVE

MAGGIE was standing in Reception, checking some notes, when practice nurse Aimee Barnes walked through the front door. 'Nice to have you back, Aimee,' she said. 'How's the arm?' The only evidence of Aimee's recently broken arm was the wrist support she wore.

'It's much better, thanks.' Aimee gave a tired smile. 'And I must say, it's nice to be back.'

'Oh, Aimee, you haven't met Fiona yet, have you?' Maggie looked up as the practice manager suddenly appeared in Reception.

Aimee shook her head and Maggie carried out the necessary introductions between the two women. As Aimee took herself off to the treatment room, Jon Turner came in through the main entrance.

'Good morning, Jon. Good weekend?' asked Maggie.

'Yes, actually.' Jon smiled. 'How about you?'

'Yes, lovely, thanks.' Maggie nodded then turned to the senior receptionist. 'Would you like to send my first patient up, please, Jackie?'

'Could I have a word, please, Dr Turner?' Fiona turned to Jon.

'Yes, of course.' The two of them disappeared in the direction of his consulting room.

'Actually, Dr Hudson,' said Jackie, 'Could *I* have a quick word with *you* before you start surgery?'

'Of course.' Maggie nodded. 'Come upstairs.' She led the way up the stairs to her consulting room then turned to face the senior receptionist. 'What is it, Jackie?' she asked as she set her case down on the desk.

'I'm not happy with the new proposals for the filing system,' said Jackie, coming straight to the point.

Maggie frowned. This was definitely not the sort of problem she wanted to contend with first thing on a Monday morning. 'Shouldn't you be telling Fiona that?' she asked.

'That's the whole point,' said Jackie tersely. 'It's Fiona who's making the proposals. Honestly, Dr Hudson, I've spent months sorting out all the filing, now she comes along and wants to change it all.'

'Well, Jackie, we have more or less given Fiona the go-ahead to carry out whatever changes she deems necessary.'

'So all my hard work counts for nothing, then?' Jackie's face had flushed a dull red and she looked as if she might be about to burst into tears.

'No, of course not,' Maggie replied hastily. She knew how sensitive the staff could be over these things and how easy it was to upset them. 'Maybe what's needed is a bit more discussion about this. I'll try and sort it out.'

'Thank you, Dr Hudson.'

'Is there anything else, Jackie?' asked Maggie when the receptionist appeared to linger.

'Do you know if Dr Neville is all right?'

Maggie frowned. 'Yes, as far as I know. Why?'

'He hasn't come in yet this morning. It's not like him to be late.'

'Maybe he's visiting a patient.'

'Yes, maybe,' Jackie agreed, then as she turned to the door she added, 'Just as long as he's all right. What I mean is, with him living alone and all that...well, we'd never know, would we, if he was taken ill or anything?'

'He was certainly all right over the weekend,' said Maggie. 'He had his children over and we joined up with them.'

'Really?' Jackie's eyes widened innocently. 'That was nice.'

'Yes, it was, very nice. Now, if that's all, I really must get on with my surgery,' said Maggie firmly.

'All right, Doctor. I'll send the first one up.' With a half-smile on her face Jackie left the room.

Maggie sighed, took off her jacket and hung it behind the door. It sounded as if what Fiona had said was true, and others really were taking an interest in hers and Sam's activities. The rumour probably was that they were living together, hence Jackie questioning her as to Sam's whereabouts that morning. She would have to make sure she scotched any such rumours before they got out of hand. And after the events of the weekend, the sooner she did so the better because it seemed as if even Sam himself had got the wrong idea.

Although, she had to admit, after that one brief episode on the beach Sam's behaviour towards her had been exactly the same as it had always been. At the time it had shocked her because there had never in the past been any indication from Sam that he wanted their relationship to change. And afterwards she had been afraid that it would change everything between them. For her part, she had never even explored the possibility of a romantic relationship with Sam because she'd never thought of him in that way. It wasn't that he wasn't attractive—he was. But before he had been Claire's husband and she had been David's wife so the possibility had never arisen.

And now that it had, she wasn't sure how she felt. There was a part of her that felt it was possibly too soon after David's death for her to be embarking on any sort of relationship, but at the same time she had to admit she had been shocked at the way her emotions had been so stirred by that moment on the beach between herself and Sam. She had wrestled with the question ever since but she had no answer other than that she was certain she wanted to retain Sam's friendship without any complications. And if they embarked upon any sort of romantic affair she was fairly certain—if all the other intrigues amongst the staff and their various relationships were anything to go by—there would be complications.

It had come as something of a surprise when Sam had confessed to having had two affairs since his split with Claire. She hadn't been aware of either of those and she didn't know how she would have reacted if she had known. Not that it was any business of hers, of course. After all, Sam was a free agent and could see whomever he chose.

A sharp rap on the door jolted her out of her reverie, and she looked up as a young woman and a little boy came into the room.

'Hello, Fran.' Maggie replaced her frown with a smile. 'Hello, Tom. How are you this morning?'

'I've got a cough,' said the little boy.

'Would you like to tell me about it?' asked Maggie.

'I cough all the time,' said Tom solemnly.

'He had a cold,' explained his mother, 'then a very chesty cough, and the cough just seems to have gone on and on for weeks.'

'He's had several chesty coughs in the past, hasn't he?' Maggie brought Tom's records up on her computer screen and studied them.

'Yes,' Fran replied. 'Always after a cold.'

'Does he get wheezy?'

'Well, I hadn't noticed it before, but this time, yes, I

have to say he is wheezy. I especially noticed it yesterday when he'd been running around with the other children.'

'I think we'd better have a listen to your chest, Tom.' Maggie picked up her stethoscope from her desk. 'Would you like to take off your fleece and lift up your T-shirt? That's right. Now, I'm afraid this may be a little bit cold, but it won't hurt.' She breathed on the end of the stethoscope before placing it on the little boy's chest.

'It tickles, Mum.' Tom squirmed. 'Can you hear anything?' he asked Maggie curiously after a moment.

'Yes.' Maggie nodded. 'I can hear your heart beating and I can hear the tubes in your chest crackling a little bit.'

'Can I listen?' asked Tom, his eyes widening.

'Of course you can.' Maggie removed the earpieces from her own ears and put them in Tom's then she placed the end of the stethoscope on the little boy's chest. He remained completely silent for a while, listening intently.

'Can you hear anything?' asked Maggie.

'I can hear a bumping noise,' Tom said at last.

'That's your heart beating,' Maggie explained. 'It's like a little pump, it pumps the blood around your body.'

'I couldn't hear any crackling,' Tom replied.

'That was a bit quieter,' Maggie admitted. 'Now, I'd like to listen to your back, please, Tom.'

The little boy turned around, his mother lifted his T-shirt and Maggie applied the stethoscope to his back.

'More crackles?' asked Tom.

'Just a few,' Maggie replied. When she had finished Fran helped Tom with his shirt and his fleece.

'I think we may be looking at asthma,' said Maggie at last, and Fran looked up quickly in alarm. 'It's all right,' she added. 'It's only mild at present but just to make sure I'm going to prescribe an inhaler for Tom. If he responds to the inhaler, it will give me a clearer picture of his problem.'

'But if it is asthma—it's always there, isn't it?' Fran looked worried. 'My friend has asthma and she always has to use medication.'

'If it is asthma, there are ways it can be controlled,' Maggie replied. 'We would give Tom an inhaler to prevent asthma attacks and we would monitor him carefully here at our own asthma clinic. One of our practice nurses takes the clinic. But at this stage all I want you to do is to use this inhaler twice a day for a month, then I'd like to see Tom again.'

'All right, Dr Hudson. Thank you.' Fran took the prescription that Maggie handed to her. 'Come on, Tom.'

'Goodbye, Tom,' said Maggie.

'Bye.'

Maggie watched as Tom and Fran left the room. She was about to press the buzzer for her next patient but on a sudden impulse she pressed the intercom switch instead. 'Oh, Katie,' she said when the receptionist replied, 'has Dr Neville come in yet?'

'No, Dr Hudson. Not yet.'

'Right. Thank you, Katie.' She flicked the switch and sat staring at the intercom. Where was Sam? It simply wasn't like him to be late for surgery.

Picking up the telephone, she dialled his home number. It rang half a dozen times then clicked onto the answering machine—Sam's voice asking the caller to leave their name and number and saying that he would return their call later. She replaced the receiver then immediately picked it up again and dialled the number of Sam's mobile phone only to find that it was switched off.

Maggie sat back in her chair and felt the first twinge of anxiety. This really wasn't like Sam. He'd probably visited a patient on his way in to work and either he'd forgotten the time, which was unlikely, or the visit had taken much longer than he'd expected, in which case Maggie would have expected him to phone in to say he was running late so that the receptionists could explain to his patients.

Maybe something was wrong with one of the children. She knew the plan had been that Claire was to have picked them up on Sunday evening, but she had phoned on Saturday while Maggie had still been there to ask if they could stay another night with Sam as she and Luke were going to the mainland to see Luke's children and wouldn't be back until late on Sunday night. The new plan was that Sam would take them home early on Monday morning so that they would have time to change and collect their gear for school. Perhaps he'd simply waited and taken them on to their respective schools on his way to work. But it still didn't explain why he hadn't phoned to say he would be late.

In a concerted attempt to put the anxiety from her mind Maggie saw a further two patients, but when a check through to Reception revealed there was still no sign or word from Sam she picked up the phone once more. After checking in the local directory, she dialled Claire's number.

Luke Tyler answered on the tenth ring.

'Luke, its Maggie Hudson.'

'Maggie, this is a surprise. What can I do for you?'

'Well, this is probably a silly question, but have you seen Sam this morning?'

'Sam? Yes, he brought the children home.'

'I thought he might have done. What time did he leave?'

'I don't know exactly. Let me check with Claire. Why, have you lost him?'

'Er…not exactly.'

'Hold on. Claire went back to bed after the children had gone. We were very late last night.'

All right for some, thought Maggie as the line went dead. She thought of Claire lying in bed then considered the enormity of her own workload for the coming day. She waited a few minutes then Claire's voice came onto the line. She sounded sleepy.

'Maggie? What's wrong?'

'I don't know that anything is wrong exactly,' Maggie replied. 'Luke tells me that Sam brought the children home this morning.'

'Yes, that's right, he did. They changed into their school clothes and he said he'd drop them off at their schools on his way into work.'

'I see. I thought it might be something like that.'

'Hasn't he arrived yet?'

'No. No, he hasn't.' Maggie tried to keep her voice as casual as possible. Somehow she didn't want Claire to know she was in the least bit anxious about Sam.

'Well, he left here just after eight o'clock. He's probably stopped off somewhere. Mind you, that's Sam all over. I never did know quite where he was or when I could expect him—'

'Yes, quite. Thank you, Claire. I'm sorry to have bothered you.' Maggie certainly didn't want to get into a conversation with Claire about Sam's shortcomings.

'Emma said they spent a lot of time with you over the weekend.' Claire obviously hadn't finished and wanted more information than her daughter had had time to give her while she'd been changing for school.

'Yes, they did. We had a lovely weekend,' said Maggie. 'But I must go now, Claire. I'm in the middle of surgery.'

She saw two more patients and was on the point of checking once more to see if Sam had now arrived when her phone rang. It was Fiona.

'Maggie, do you have a patient with you?'

'No. Not at the moment, Fiona.'

'I've just had a call from the police.'

'The police…?' Maggie's heart turned over. Normally she would have thought nothing of hearing that the police had phoned because there were many occasions when the doctors and the local police were in contact. 'What did they want?' she asked.

'They said they'd had a call from a member of the public who'd seen Sam's car parked on the cliffs on the coast road. Apparently there was no sign of Sam and they'd said it looked as if the car had been abandoned there. The police said they'd keep us informed… Maggie, are you still there?'

'Yes. I'm still here.'

'There's probably a perfectly reasonable explanation and they said not to worry.'

Not to worry. She replaced the receiver. Her heart was thumping. Where was Sam? Why would his car be abandoned on the coast road? What had happened to him? That particular stretch of road was notorious for accidents and there had been many fatalities, including suicides, at the spot over the years. But not Sam. Surely not Sam.

Suddenly Maggie felt as if cold hands had wrapped themselves around her heart. If anything had happened to Sam she didn't know what she'd do. Since David's death he'd been her rock, her mainstay, but what of Sam himself? What had she really known about his state of mind over the past year? She'd known he'd been devastated when his marriage had broken up but he'd appeared to get over that to some extent or at least he'd given that impression.

But what if he hadn't? What if he'd been depressed and none of them had noticed?

He'd helped her to get over David's death but David had been his best friend. Had David's death on top of his own marriage break-up simply been too much for him? But if that were so, surely his partners should have seen the signs. They were doctors, for heaven's sake, and if Jon hadn't seen it then she should have done. She was his friend. Had she quite simply been so wrapped up in her own affairs that she'd been totally insensitive to the needs of those closest to her? But if something had happened to Sam, what could have triggered it? Why now? He'd seemed so happy at the weekend. Why, he'd even... Oh, heavens! Her hand flew to her mouth as she recalled that moment of tenderness between them and of how she'd then rejected him. Had that proved to be the final straw? Had it tipped him over the edge?

With a strangled cry Maggie jumped to her feet and moved to the door, tugging it open. She couldn't just sit there, waiting for something to happen. She had to do something. She didn't know what. She only knew that Sam could be in trouble and might need her help.

The corridor outside her consulting room was deserted and she sped down the stairs into Reception. There was the usual chaotic Monday morning crowd of patients all milling around the desk, but Maggie hardly saw them, neither was she aware that Jackie called out to her. She wasn't even really sure where she was going. She only had a vague idea that she had to go out onto the coast road where Sam's car had been seen.

She pulled open the double doors of the main entrance

then collided head-on with someone coming into the building. So intent was she in her flight that she hardly noticed who it was.

'Sorry!' she gasped. The person grasped her arms to steady her and with a sudden shock of recognition she realised it was Sam.

'Sam!' She stared at him wildly.

'Maggie?' He grinned. 'Whatever's wrong? Where's the fire?'

'Whatever's wrong...?' She shook her head in bewilderment then as realisation washed over her that it was actually Sam and that he seemed to be all right, she felt a sudden unreasonable surge of anger at her own somewhat unprofessional response to the situation.

'Where have you been?' she demanded, and to her horror she found herself thumping his chest with both her fists.

'Hey, what is this?' He held her at arm's length.

'I thought something had happened to you,' she cried, aware that tears had sprung to her eyes. 'I thought you were dead!'

'Dead?' He stared at her. 'Whatever made you think that?'

'You were so late...then the police phoned. They said...they said your car had been seen up on the cliffs but there was no sign of you.' She was aware that her voice had a touch of hysteria in it, but she seemed unable to control it.

'That's right,' Sam replied cheerfully. 'I was chasing old Percy North's dog.'

'You were chasing a dog?' Maggie gaped at him, unsure whether to laugh or cry.

'Hey, you really are upset, aren't you?' Sam lowered his head and tried to look into her eyes. 'Come on, let's get inside.' He stared past her into the crowded reception area where people had turned and were staring in open curiosity. 'On second thoughts, we'll go in the back way.'

With Sam's arm around her, they made their way round the building to the rear entrance, let themselves in and managed to get up the stairs and into Maggie's consulting room without encountering anyone else. Maggie's heart was still thumping uncomfortably as she sank down into her chair. Sam perched on her desk, looking down at her with a look of puzzled concern on his face.

'Are you going to tell me what this is all about?' he asked at last.

'I would think it should be me asking that question,' Maggie replied.

'Well, I appreciate all the concern, I really do, but, like I say, I was only helping Percy rescue Nipper, his dog...'

'Did you see the police?' asked Maggie suddenly.

'No, should I have done?'

'Well, I gathered that when your car was reported abandoned on the cliffs they were going up there to investigate.'

'They certainly hadn't arrived before I left. Perhaps I should give them a ring and tell them there's no need to launch a search party.' Sam gave a dry chuckle but before he could carry out his intention Maggie's phone rang. She lifted the handset. It was Fiona.

'I have the police on the other line, Maggie.'

'Sam's here, Fiona.'

'So I understand—the girls saw you come upstairs. The police want to speak to him.'

Wordlessly Maggie passed the receiver to Sam, who stood up and walked to the window. Vaguely as she struggled to get her own emotions under control, she heard him reassuring the police that he was all right and thanking them for their concern.

When at last he put the phone down he glanced at his watch. 'I actually had no idea I was so late,' he said. Looking at Maggie, he went on, 'I'm sorry, Maggie. I really am. I should have phoned to say where I was and what was happening.'

'What did happen exactly?' she asked.

'I dropped the children off at their schools and as I was driving back along the coast road I saw old Percy North. He was quite near the cliff edge and he appeared agitated. He was running about and waving his arms. He'd seen my car approaching and he was trying to attract my attention. Anyway, I stopped and ran across the field to join him. He told me he and his dog Nipper had been walking along the clifftop. Nipper had been chasing rabbits when he'd suddenly disappeared over the edge. Percy could hear him whimpering but apparently couldn't see him. We went to have a look and realised that the dog was trapped on a ledge in some thick undergrowth which had broken his fall. I decided that if I was careful I could climb down and rescue him.'

'Didn't it occur to you to call the coastguard?' asked Maggie.

'With hindsight, I suppose that's what I should have done,' Sam agreed sheepishly. 'But at the time I simply thought I could retrieve him with the minimum of fuss.'

'And did you?' asked Maggie.

'Eventually. Yes.' Sam nodded. 'But it was more hazardous than I'd thought. It was very sticky underfoot after all the rain we've had and it was a job to keep my balance. It was also high tide and the surf was crashing about on the rocks below. Still...' he shrugged '...everything was

OK in the end and Nipper is back safe and sound with his master.'

'I expect you'll have fresh produce for all time now,' said Maggie weakly.

'Quite.' Sam grinned then grew serious again. 'Maggie?'

'Yes?'

'Tell me, I'm curious. Just what exactly did you think had happened to me?'

'I didn't know.' She shook her head then in an attempt to explain she said, 'For a start it wasn't like you to be so late without letting anyone know. I'd rung your home number, then your mobile—I'd even rung Claire.'

'Claire?' Sam looked up sharply. 'You rang Claire?'

'Yes.'

'What did you do that for?'

'Well, I knew you would have gone there first with the children. I just wondered what time you left.'

'I bet Claire loved the fact that you couldn't track me down.'

Maggie shrugged helplessly. 'Just after that the police phoned…and then…well, then I really didn't know what to think…'

'You thought I'd had an accident?'

'Like I say, I didn't know what to think. For your car to have been seen abandoned up there on that cliff road…'

Sam stared at her. 'You didn't think I'd topped myself?' he asked incredulously.

'No. Of course not,' she said quickly, then with a gesture she added, 'I don't know, Sam… I don't know what I thought. I guess I panicked which, I know, is totally unforgivable. We doctors aren't supposed to be prone to such shows of emotion, are we?'

'I didn't know you cared so much, Maggie.'

'Of course I do.' She looked up into his face. 'Of course I do, Sam. If anything happened to you I really don't know what I'd do. I used to believe the unthinkable couldn't happen. But it did happen once and I know it could happen again... And quite honestly I don't think I could bear it...' Her voice cracked.

'Oh, Maggie.' Stepping forward, he took her hands then drew her up into his arms and held her close in a warm hug.

'Thank God you're safe, Sam.' Her voice was shaky as for the second time in the space of a couple of days she found herself in his arms. Now, as then, she felt intensely aware of him, of the beating of his heart, the slight roughness of his jaw and the scent of him—his aftershave, the soap he used and, more significantly, the very maleness of him. It was something that had been unfamiliar of late—this closeness, this raw intimacy with a man—and once again Maggie felt the stirring of some emotion deep inside, that half-forgotten emotion once known as desire.

They remained that way, clasped in each other's arms, for a long time, only drawing apart when the intercom sounded. Leaning across the desk, Maggie weakly flicked the switch. Afterwards she was to wonder what might have happened if that interruption hadn't come. Had Sam felt what she had? If so, would he have kissed her? And if he had, how would she have reacted? Would she have pushed him away as she had before or would she have responded to that brief flare of passion? There was no way of knowing, but Maggie had the distinct impression that this time she might have found Sam just too difficult to resist.

'Dr Hudson, is Dr Neville with you?'

'Yes, Jackie, he is.'

'There are an awful lot of patients waiting down here

both for Dr Neville and for you. We aren't sure what we should be telling them.'

It was Sam who answered. 'Jackie? Would you apologise to them for the delay this morning, which was unavoidable, and tell them that both Dr Hudson and myself will resume surgeries immediately?'

'Very well, Dr Neville. Anything you say.'

As he switched off the intercom Sam pulled a face. 'I guess we've supplied ample speculation to keep them all going for the next month at least,' he said with a wry smile.

'Oh, at least.' Maggie answered casually enough but as Sam squeezed her hand then left her room she found she was still trembling.

CHAPTER SIX

SAM pressed the buzzer for his first patient. Running as late as this was really not the best way to be starting a Monday morning. The events of the past couple of hours had been taxing to say the least; there was mud on his trousers and he felt hot and dishevelled after scrabbling halfway down the cliff. Really, he would have liked nothing better than to have slipped back home and showered and changed but there was no time. And then there had been Maggie's unexpected reaction to what had happened. He wanted time to think about that but he knew that time wasn't now and it would have to wait as he faced the demands of the day and a busy surgery.

'Come in.' He looked up quickly calling out in response to a sudden knock on his door. 'Nigel, good morning,' he added as a man in his early forties came into the room. 'Come in and take a seat, please.'

The man, Nigel Greening, bespectacled, balding and neatly dressed in tweed jacket and grey trousers, was the headmaster of the local primary school and knew Sam well both socially and professionally. 'Good morning, Sam,' he said as he sat down.

'Sorry to have kept you waiting.'

'I'm sure there was a very good reason.'

'There was,' Sam replied briskly. 'Now, how may I help you?'

'I've developed a rash,' Nigel Greening replied. 'It's quite painful and it's driving me mad. I thought I'd better get it checked out before I come into contact with any of the children. It's on my side,' he added, indicating his left side.

'Any other symptoms?' asked Sam.

'Well, if I'm honest, I haven't felt at all well over the weekend. I've been hot and shivery at the same time, as if I was coming down with a dose of flu. Once or twice I felt nauseous. The itching from the rash has kept me awake and this morning, I have to say, it's quite painful.'

'Let's take a look at this rash.' Sam stood up while Nigel, wincing with pain, took off his jacket, loosened his tie and began to unbutton his shirt.

Carefully Sam inspected the red blister-like spots, which covered a largish area on Nigel's trunk and abdomen. Then he checked his patient's pulse and temperature, both of which were slightly raised.

'I'm afraid, Nigel, that you have shingles,' he said at last.

'Good God! I thought only elderly people got shingles.' Looking faintly stunned, the headmaster sat down again.

'Not at all. It can affect any age group.'

'Some of the children at school have had chickenpox recently. Could I have caught it from them?' asked Nigel anxiously.

Sam shook his head. 'No,' he said. 'It doesn't happen like that. But you're right that it's connected to chickenpox. You will have had chickenpox yourself at some point in the past, probably when you were a child.'

'That's right, I did,' Nigel agreed.

'The virus remains dormant, sometimes for many years, but if your immune system is under attack for any reason it can flare up again, this time as shingles,' Sam explained. 'It's a painful condition and you'll need to take some time off work and rest. I'll prescribe some medication which has proved to be very effective in the treatment of shingles.'

Sam washed his hands then sat down at his desk and brought up Nigel's medication chart on his computer screen. 'I'll want to see you again in a week's time,' he said as he waited for the prescription to print, 'but I think you'll find that the condition will respond pretty quickly to the medication.'

'There was something else I was going to mention to you,' said Nigel as he took the prescription and Sam wrote out a sickness certificate. 'It's a bit delicate and concerns a child at school. I have nothing really specific to go on, just that a class teacher is worried by a change in the child's behaviour.'

'Is the child a patient of mine?'

'I'm not certain—although he would certainly be registered with this practice. But his mother is an employee of yours.'

'Really?' Sam looked up in surprise.

'Yes. The child is Joshua Barnes.'

'Aimee Barnes's son?'

'Yes.' Nigel nodded then once again winced with pain as he struggled into his jacket.

'Can you say why the teacher was concerned?' asked Sam.

'Not really. As I say, it was simply a hunch because of a change in behaviour.'

'So what was the change? Has he become disruptive?'

'No, the reverse, I think. Apparently he's become very withdrawn. I thought I'd mention it, especially now that I'm to be off work and unable to keep an eye on the situation. I may be speaking out of turn or there may be nothing at all to worry about.'

'In which case there's no harm done,' said Sam. 'Leave it with me. I'll make a few discreet enquiries.'

'Thanks, Sam.'

'Now, get yourself off home and rest.'

As Nigel left the room Sam sat for a moment, drumming his fingers on the desk, deep in thought. So often, as a doctor, he was given pieces of information in confidence on which he was required to make a decision as to whether or not any further action should be taken. After a moment he pressed a couple of keys on the computer, bringing Joshua Barnes's details to the screen. The entire Barnes family was registered with Maggie and there was nothing significant about Joshua's notes. He appeared to be a perfectly normal eight-year-old boy with the usual number of medical attendances for childhood ailments. His mother Aimee had been an employee for several years as a part-time practice nurse and her medical chart proved to be fairly standard, the most recent entry being for her broken arm, an injury sustained falling from her bicycle.

There were two other children, a girl older than Joshua by three years and a younger boy. The girl had suffered with dyslexia and mild learning difficulties and the boy was asthmatic. Aimee's husband, Denis, the manager at the local supermarket, was also a volunteer member of the fire brigade and there was next to nothing on his medical records.

Sam decided to have a word with Maggie about the situation and made a brief note to that effect on the jotter on his desk, then he pressed the buzzer for his next patient.

'That's the last one, Dr Hudson.'

'Thanks, Katie.' With a sigh of relief Maggie stretched then stood up. The events of the morning had drained her and she was more than pleased that her surgery was over. A faint niggle over her left eye was threatening to escalate into a full-scale headache and this, she knew, was as a direct result of the tension she'd felt over Sam.

Her reaction to the situation had surprised her and the more she'd thought about it since, the more she realised that she had, of course, overreacted. However, Sam had been very late and that together with the fact that he hadn't let anyone know, had been totally uncharacteristic of him. That he'd merely been helping out someone in distress and that someone a patient who would have expected Sam's help was neither here nor there because she'd been unaware of that at the time. And nothing altered the fact that there could have been a crisis. Sam could have been in real danger. He'd said himself that the ground had been wet and slippery. He could have missed his footing and slid down the cliff face, crashing onto the rocks below.

She shuddered at the very thought. He wouldn't have been the first to fall to his death from those cliffs. The thought of losing Sam in such a fashion simply didn't bear thinking about—the thought of losing Sam at all didn't bear thinking about.

Giving herself a little shake, Maggie pulled her cardigan more closely around her and, leaving her room, made her way along the corridor to the staffroom.

Jon was already in the room, sitting in one of the easy chairs by the window, his legs crossed, a mug of coffee in one hand, a medical journal in the other. He looked up as Maggie came into the room. 'Hello,' he said, and from the inflexion in his voice Maggie knew he was curious.

'Hi, Jon.' Casually she crossed the room and poured herself a coffee.

'What was all that fuss about this morning?'

'Fuss?' Deliberately she remained vague.

'Yes, all those hordes in Reception, waiting for Sam.'

'Oh, *that* fuss.'

'Why was he so late?' Jon was openly curious now.

'He was rescuing a dog from the clifftop.'

'A dog?' Jon's expression was comical.

'Yes, a dog. That's all it was. It was no big deal.'

'OK, so why was there so much panic?'

'Panic? Was there?'

'From the look on your face when you passed my door, I thought at the very least someone had been murdered, and then I heard the girls say something about the police out searching for Sam.'

'It was nothing, Jon. Believe me, it was nothing,' said Maggie firmly. 'It could have been, but it wasn't...' She trailed off as the staffroom door suddenly opened and Sam himself appeared. He paused for a moment and looked from Maggie to Jon then back to Maggie again as from their abrupt silence it must have been apparent that they'd been talking about him.

'Well, here he is,' said Jon, breaking the silence, 'the man of the moment. How does it feel to be a hero, Sam?'

'I don't know,' Sam replied. 'I've never been one.'

'Oh, I don't know.' Jon grinned. 'I dare say there's a certain dog who'll hail you as his hero till the end of his days.'

Sam shrugged and, crossing the room, poured a coffee.

'Whose was the dog anyway?' asked Jon. 'Anyone we know?'

'Actually,' said Sam, taking a sip of his coffee, 'it was old Percy's dog.'

'Percy?' Jon laughed. 'If you were going to risk life and limb, I'd have thought you could have found some fair damsel who needed your services.'

'I should be so lucky.' Sam smiled while Jon, still chuckling to himself, drained his mug, stood up and strolled from the room, his journal under his arm.

'He never changes, does he?' said Maggie with a sigh.

Sam wryly shook his head. Taking another sip, he said, 'I'm glad I've caught you on your own, Maggie.'

'Problems?' she asked, frowning. She wasn't sure she could cope with anything more that morning.

'I'm not sure. I had Nigel Greening in this morning.' Sam paused, as if considering how to continue. 'He happened to mention that one of his staff was concerned about young Joshua Barnes.'

'Aimee's Joshua? Why, what's wrong with him?'

'Not certain. A change in behaviour patterns, Nigel said.'

'What sort of change?'

'He's become withdrawn apparently.'

'I wonder what's caused that,' said Maggie slowly. 'It doesn't sound like Joshua, I have to say.'

'The family is registered with you, isn't it?' asked Sam, and when Maggie nodded he went on, 'Were you aware of any problems?'

'No, not really,' she replied. 'I certainly didn't think there were any marital problems. In fact, I thought we'd already observed that Aimee's was the only normal marriage amongst us.'

'That's true.' Sam sighed. 'On the other hand, you can never be sure about these things.'

'Maybe Joshua is being bullied at school,' said Maggie slowly.

'Maybe,' Sam agreed. 'In which case, I would imagine that now his teacher has noticed his behaviour, she would be on the lookout for anything like that.'

Maggie was silent for a moment, her hands drawing

comfort from the warmth of her mug. 'Would you like me to have a word with Aimee?' she asked at last.

'Well, maybe not directly, but perhaps in a roundabout way in conversation. I feel something has to be done, especially as Nigel has gone to the trouble to draw it to our attention. On the other hand, it could be delicate with Aimee working for us.'

'I'll see what I can do.' Rising to her feet, Maggie drained her mug then moved towards the door. 'I must get on,' she said. 'I have a cervical smear clinic before lunch.'

'Maggie,' said Sam as she reached the door.

She stopped, one hand on the door handle. 'Yes?' she asked, in that instant somehow fearing that what he might be about to say would allude to her near hysterical behaviour of earlier.

'I'm sorry I put you through that anxiety this morning.'

'It's all right, Sam. Really it is. I guess I just overreacted, that's all.'

'Even so.' He shrugged. 'I should have thought. I suppose I never considered that anyone would actually worry about me to such an extent.'

'Well, now you know.' She gave a rueful smile. 'We're very fond of you, Sam—you must have known that.'

'We?' he raised his eyebrows questioningly.

'Yes, me…and the children…' She became flustered by something in his eyes. 'And all of us here, of course,' she added.

'Oh, I see.' It was his turn to give a rueful grin. As he stood up he said, 'It was a good weekend, wasn't it?'

'Yes, it was. And I haven't even got around to thanking you. It was lovely, Sam, and I know my two thoroughly enjoyed themselves.'

'Even Jessica?'

'Even Jessica,' Maggie replied firmly.

'I was afraid she was beginning to consider herself beyond the simple pleasures of walks and picnics.'

'In theory maybe. But the reality usually proves her wrong. How about your two?'

'Oh, they had a whale of a time. Didn't want to go home, actually. Richard especially.'

'It must be terribly hard.'

'Yes, for me as well.'

'I *meant* for you. I couldn't imagine it.' Maggie shook her head. 'I doubt if I'd cope.'

'Yes, you would.' Sam sighed. 'You cope because you have to. I have no choice.'

'Have you thought about applying for custody?'

'What, and turning their world upside down again simply for my benefit?'

'It could turn out to be for their benefit as well.'

'I don't know.' Sam shook his head. 'I have wondered about approaching Claire about them spending more time with me.'

'Would she object to that?'

Sam gave a short laugh. 'With Claire, who knows?'

'If it were me, I don't think I'd object,' said Maggie as Sam stood back for her to precede him through the door.

'Ah,' he said, 'but Claire isn't you, Maggie.'

It was the first time he'd ever made any sort of comparison between herself and Claire, and while its only implication was that she would be more reasonable than Claire there was something in the way he said it that left Maggie lost for words.

'I'll walk down with you,' Sam said. 'I have a couple of house calls to make.'

Together they left the staffroom and made their way along the corridor and down the stairs. The reception and the waiting area had cleared, with just a handful of patients presumably waiting for various clinics. Sam collected his notes from Reception and headed for the door, ready to do his house visits, while Maggie made her way to the treatment room where she found Aimee setting out the trolley and instruments in readiness for the smear clinic.

'How many patients do we have booked in, Aimee?' Maggie asked as she donned a white surgical coat.

'Six.' Aimee replied. 'Shall I call the first one?'

'Yes, please, do.' As Aimee hurried out of the room Maggie found herself wondering what the problem could be relating to her colleague's young son. She knew from experience, her own as well as her professional involvement, that young children could be constantly up and down in their behaviour patterns, but she felt that in Joshua's case it must have constituted something particularly noticeable for his headmaster to have felt it necessary to bring it to the attention of the medical team.

She had no further opportunity for speculation at that time, however, because Aimee returned to the treatment room almost immediately with the first of their patients for a cervical smear. This was a young woman in her early twenties who had been on the Pill for seven years and had had several sexual partners. Maggie had recently been treating her for a chlamydial infection which was sexually transmitted. Each time she saw her she warned her of the dangers of unprotected sex but she felt her warnings fell on deaf ears. She'd even had her doubts that the young woman would attend for her routine smear check.

Maggie and Aimee worked steadily through the list and when they were left with just one more patient to see Maggie asked Aimee how she had coped with her first morning back at work.

'Fine.' Aimee smiled brightly.

'Arm not aching?' Maggie glanced down at Aimee's left arm with its support bandage.

'A bit,' Aimee admitted, 'but, then, it does—most of the time if I'm honest. But it is getting less,' she added hastily.

'You mustn't overdo it,' said Maggie. She paused. 'How about at home?'

'At home?' Aimee frowned. 'How do you mean?'

'Well, do you get plenty of help?'

'Oh, well, you know what kids are like. They start off helping then there's always something more important, like football practice or watching the latest video.'

'And Denis, does he help?'

'Oh, yes, Denis is marvellous. I'm very lucky there.'

'Good. Right, let's call in Mrs Hammond and afterwards we can go to lunch.'

Aimee went off to call their last patient, leaving Maggie to muse over their conversation. It certainly hadn't sounded as if Aimee's was a family with problems—in fact, it sounded remarkably normal and a good deal better than many. If there was a problem, it was either very well concealed or it seemed to point to the child's behaviour being in direct relation to some factor outside the home, probably at school, which left Maggie thinking that maybe it needed approaching from a different angle.

'Mum, can we have a bonfire party?'

It was later that same day and Maggie, Jessica, William and Ingrid had just finished supper.

'Oh, yes!' It was William who responded to his sister's request. 'That would be cool.'

'I don't know,' said Maggie dubiously.

'*Please.* We haven't had a party for absolutely ages.' Jessica put on her best wheedling tones.

'There's been a very good reason for that, Jessica,' said Maggie quietly.

'Yes, I know.' Jessica pouted. 'But Daddy loved parties, you know he did, and I know he wouldn't want us to mope about for ever and not have any fun.'

'That's true,' Maggie agreed, 'but I wasn't aware that we were moping exactly.'

'So we can have the party, then?' Jessica's eyes shone. 'We could ask Richard and Emma and I would ask Sophie and Max. Max Price—I could ask him, couldn't I?'

'Jackie's son?' Maggie frowned. 'Yes, I suppose so…'

'So we can, then?'

'Well, I guess it is time we returned some hospitality,' said Maggie. 'But I'm not sure about a bonfire party…'

'Oh, it would be brill!' cried William. 'D'you remember that bonfire party we had before and…and Daddy set off all those Catherine wheels at once?'

Maggie blinked and nodded. 'Yes,' she said, 'of course I do. But the whole point was that Daddy was here then to set off the fireworks.'

'Sam would do it,' said Jessica airily.

'Or Josh Barnes's dad,' said William solemnly. 'He's a fireman.'

'Is Josh a special friend of yours?' asked Maggie curiously.

'Of course he is,' William replied.

'Well, we'll see,' said Maggie. The children clattered down from the table and disappeared to their rooms to complete their homework. Maggie sat on at the table for a moment, reflecting on how strange life could be sometimes. There she'd been all day wondering how she could make some discreet enquiries about Joshua Barnes and what might be bothering him, and all the time he and William were friends. She'd known they were in the same year at school, of course, but she hadn't realised they were friends as she'd hardly heard William mention Joshua before.

Maybe this bonfire party wouldn't be a bad idea after all. Possibly they could include the staff and their families. Social contact was important amongst the staff as far as Maggie was concerned, and this time it was long overdue. Jon would probably protest and even Sam might not be completely whole-hearted, but the more Maggie thought about it the more she thought that her daughter might have hit on a good idea.

'What do you think about this bonfire party, Ingrid?' she asked as they cleared the supper table.

'I think it sounds like a wonderful idea,' Ingrid replied. 'Jessica's right—this house needs fun and laughter again.'

'I was just thinking,' Maggie went on slowly. 'We could make it a party for the staff and their families—they've all been so good to me in the last year—and the children could ask their friends from school.'

'I'll help with the food,' said Ingrid enthusiastically. 'We have a little while yet. I could start baking and we could freeze things—strudel, apple cake, poacher's pie and things like that.'

'And on the night we could roast chestnuts and bake potatoes and we could set up the barbecue in the barn and Sam could barbecue steaks and sausages—he's brilliant at that,' said Maggie. 'D'you know, Ingrid, this idea is really beginning to grow on me.'

'Well, I think it's a wonderful idea,' said Ingrid. She began to stack the dishwasher then she paused and looked up. 'I was in the butcher's shop this afternoon and they were all talking about Dr Neville rescuing Percy's dog. That was marvellous, wasn't it?'

'Yes, it was,' Maggie agreed.

'But they were also saying that you were really angry with Dr Neville because he was so late for surgery. Was that right?'

'Not entirely, no.'

'I didn't think it could be. I didn't comment, of course. I never do when it's anything to do with the family or the practice, but I still didn't think it could be right.' Ingrid paused again as if waiting for Maggie to say more.

'I was angry, yes,' Maggie said at last, 'but not because Dr Neville was late. Neither was it because he had stopped to rescue Percy's dog—I was glad he was able to help. No, I was upset because I didn't know where he was…and then the police phoned and said his car had been spotted and I thought…I thought… Oh, I don't know what I thought.'

'You thought something had happened to him.'

'Well, yes, I suppose I did.'

'And that really would have been the end of the world, wouldn't it?' said Ingrid bluntly.

Maggie gave a deep sigh. 'Yes, Ingrid,' she admitted at last, 'I do believe it would have been.'

'Maybe I should have said something in the butcher's when they were all gossiping…'

'No, you did right not to,' said Maggie. In a concentrated effort to change the subject, she went on, 'Oh, Ingrid, I've been meaning to ask—how is your mother?'

'She's feeling a lot better since you put her on those steroid tablets, Maggie.'

'I thought she would. That's good,' Maggie replied.

'She didn't want to take them, you know.'

'No, I know she didn't. The thing will be to make sure she doesn't stop taking them as she starts feeling better.'

'I'll try and make sure she doesn't do that,' Ingrid replied. 'Now, I can finish clearing up here. I'm sure you can find something else to do.'

'Thanks,' Maggie replied. 'Actually, I'm very tired. I'm going to have a bath, and then I think I'll get to bed.'

She soaked for a long time in a hot, scented bath, relaxing as she felt the stresses and strains of the day float away. But later when she was in bed she found for some reason she couldn't get Sam out of her mind, and quite suddenly she had a strong urge to phone him. But what possible reason could she give for phoning him so late in the evening? She considered for a moment and then she had the solution—she could tell him about the party.

He answered his phone on the second ring almost as if he'd been expecting a call.

'Hello, Sam—it's Maggie.'

'Maggie.' His voice softened as it slipped out of doctor mode. 'This is a surprise.' Then with an edge of concern, he asked, 'Is there anything wrong?'

'No, everything's fine,' she replied quickly. 'I'm sorry...it's late. In fact, I hadn't realised how late,' she added, glancing at her bedside clock and realising with a little start that it was well after midnight. 'You weren't asleep, were you?'

'No. I'm in bed,' he admitted. 'Well, on the bed, to be precise—I've just got out of the shower—but I wasn't asleep. I would have thought you'd have been in bed at this time of night.'

'Oh, I am,' she replied quickly. 'I should have rung you earlier but what with one thing and another I got sidetracked—you know how it is.'

'Only too well,' he agreed. 'So, what can I do for you?' he added softly.

Suddenly there seemed something incredibly intimate about Sam lying on his bed and she in hers, and he asking her what he could do for her. Her pulse quickened slightly at the thought but she ignored it, attempting instead to bring her thoughts back to what she'd been going to tell him. Settling herself more comfortably, she tucked the phone in snugly against her shoulder. 'It's Jessica,' she said at last. 'She wants a party.'

'What sort of party?'

'A bonfire party.'

'Well, I guess that shouldn't be too difficult to arrange,' said Sam slowly. 'A few of her school friends, hot dogs, one or two sparklers—is that the sort of thing?'

'Er, not quite. That may have been the original idea but it's grown a bit since then.'

Sam chuckled, a deep rich sound that touched a chord in Maggie and made her smile. She could just picture him lying on his bed in his bathrobe his hair still damp from the shower and on his face that lazy, heavy-lidded smile that she knew so well. 'I might have known it wouldn't be anything simple, coming from Jessica,' he said. 'So what does she want—a huge firework display and a disco?'

'Not quite.' Maggie found herself laughing. 'And in all fairness it wasn't all Jessica. The idea was certainly hers but once she and William talked me into it I found myself thinking it might be a good opportunity to return some hospitality by making it a party for the practice—you know, spouses and children, that sort of thing. What do you think?'

'Sounds great to me.'

'Ingrid was all for it—saw it as an excuse for a marathon bake-up. I wasn't sure at first. It'll be the first gathering we've had at Mill House since…well, since…' She was silent for a long moment. 'I was wondering,' she said, 'would you help me to host it?'

'Of course I will.' His reply was instantaneous.

'Thanks, Sam. We'll talk about the details some other time but I just wanted to get your reaction first before we all got too carried away.'

'There's no problem as far as I'm concerned.' He paused. 'Were you all right after all that trauma this morning?'

'Yes, I'm fine,' she replied, 'but, would you believe, according to Ingrid the story had even reached the butcher's shop in the village—about how you'd risked your neck to save Percy's dog and how I was angry with you for being late for surgery.'

'I don't doubt it.' He chuckled again.

'Anyway, Sam, I mustn't keep you any longer, I'll let you get to sleep.'

'I'm not in any hurry—it isn't often these days that I get phone calls from a lady at this time of night.'

Something in his tone left her not knowing quite what to say next, and in the end, helplessly, she said, 'Well, you may not be tired, but if I don't get some sleep soon I'll be late tomorrow morning. And if that happens, between the two of us we really will be getting the surgery a bad name.'

'I'd better let you go, then.' Maggie thought she detected a definite trace of reluctance in his voice. 'Goodnight, Maggie.'

'Goodnight, Sam.'

She hung up and settled down to sleep, but in spite of the fact that previously she'd felt tired she now found it impossible to get to sleep because for some obscure reason all she could see in her mind's eye was a picture of Sam as he lay on his bed, and all she could think about was the moment she'd realised that he was safe and once again he'd held her in his arms.

CHAPTER SEVEN

JESSICA'S idea for a bonfire party rapidly caught on and Maggie's idea to extend it to a party for practice staff and their families was hailed with enthusiasm by everyone. Sam, as he'd already indicated, was all for the party and offered to help in any way he could. Even Jon seemed taken by the idea, which surprised Maggie.

'Richard and Emma will be able to come, won't they?' Maggie asked Sam. It was the following Saturday and Sam had stopped by Mill House on his way home from a shopping expedition. Coffee was bubbling merrily in the percolator and Ingrid had made a batch of cherry buns, which were cooling on a rack on the kitchen table.

'I hope so,' Sam replied. 'I did mention it to Emma the last time I spoke to her but I'll remind her again.'

'It sounds like all the staff are coming.'

'You said that as if you doubted they would,' said Sam, eyeing the cherry buns.

'Well, I did wonder if it would be everyone's cup of tea. It's a pretty mixed bunch we have now, you know.' Taking two mugs from the cupboard, Maggie began to pour the coffee. 'I did wonder whether to ask Denis Barnes if he would set the fireworks off as he's in the fire service.'

'Good idea,' Sam agreed. 'That's not the sort of thing that should be left to chance, especially with a large party. You can just imagine the headlines, can't you, if something went wrong? Firework Accident at Doctors' Party.'

'Don't!' Maggie shuddered. 'It doesn't bear thinking about.'

'Talking of the Barneses,' said Sam after a moment, 'is there any more info on Josh?'

Maggie shook her head. 'No, nothing. I tried asking William about Josh in a roundabout sort of way but I fear eight-year-olds aren't the best source of information over matters like that. I also asked Aimee in passing if she was coping and she assured me everything was fine. I have to say I'm beginning to think that Josh's teacher may have imagined the whole thing.'

'Well, let's hope she did. But there must have been a certain amount of concern for Nigel to get involved.'

'Tell you what,' said Maggie, 'I'll go to the house and see Denis about the fireworks. Sometimes seeing a family on their home ground gives a much better picture than seeing them individually, whether at work or at school, and at least that would give me a legitimate reason.'

'Good idea.'

'Now, would you like one of Ingrid's cherry buns?'

'I thought you'd never ask,' Sam replied with a sigh.

'Sam.' William suddenly appeared in the kitchen doorway. 'Will you help us to make a Guy Fawkes?'

Sam nodded, his mouth full of cherry bun.

'Have you got any old clothes we could use?'

Sam swallowed. 'That was delicious. Yes, Wills, old chap, I'm sure I can find something.'

'Oh, cool.' William turned and dashed out of the kitchen. 'Jess,' he yelled, 'Sam says he'll help us to make a Guy.'

'You're very good to them, Sam,' said Maggie quietly.

'Not at all.' Sam shook his head. 'The pleasure's all mine, I can assure you. It's just the sort of thing I'd be doing with my two if they lived with me.'

                          *   *   *

Maggie's opportunity to visit the Barnes household came sooner than she thought for on the very next day, which happened to be her Sunday on call, she found herself on the road where they lived, having just visited an elderly patient. Leaving the patient's house, she drove the short distance to the Barnes home and for a few moments sat outside, looking up at the house. Because it was a Sunday, she wondered whether or not she should go in. It was a semi-detached, red-brick house built in the 1930s like so many others in the same area of the west Wight. The garden was neatly kept with a small lawn and clumps of Michaelmas daisies and a few dark red wallflowers in the borders. There were fresh white net curtains at all the front windows and two cars were parked on the drive—Aimee's dark green Vauxhall and a larger, pale blue Ford, presumably her husband's.

Maybe Sunday was the best day to call after all, Maggie thought. At least she could be more certain of finding the family at home.

Climbing out of her car, she locked it, approached the house and rang the doorbell. Joshua's older sister, Melanie, opened the door almost immediately. She stared at Maggie as if she were someone who had just arrived from another planet.

'Who is it?' called a voice, which Maggie recognised as Aimee's.

'It's the doctor,' Melanie shouted back.

'The doctor…?' Aimee appeared in the hallway behind Melanie. 'Oh, Maggie!' she said. 'This is a surprise.'

'Hello, Aimee,' Maggie replied brightly. 'I'm sorry to bother you on a Sunday but I was passing the house—'

'Is there anything wrong?' Aimee frowned and glanced over Maggie's shoulder.

'No, not at all. Actually, it was your husband I wanted to see.'

'Denis?'

'Yes, is he at home?'

'He's in the back garden,' said Melanie.

'You'd better come in,' said Aimee, 'and I'll call him.'

'I could go and find him in the garden if you like.' Maggie stepped into the hall and Aimee closed the front door behind her.

'No. No, I'll fetch him. Perhaps you'd like to wait in here.' Aimee opened a door to the left of the front door and Maggie found herself in a sitting room which, considering this was a household with three children, was immaculately tidy. She found herself wishing that her own children were half as tidy. Weekends at Mill House when Ingrid was invariably off duty tended to look as if a whirlwind had struck the place.

There were framed photographs on a large oak wall unit and Maggie moved over for a closer look. There was a wedding photograph of a very young-looking Aimee and Denis and photographs of all three children—as babies, and school photos taken at various stages.

'Dr Hudson?' She'd become so engrossed in the photographs that she hadn't heard anyone come into the room. She spun round to find Denis in the doorway.

'Oh, Denis, hello. I was just admiring these pictures of the children.'

'Handsome bunch, aren't they? Must take after their old man.' He laughed, revealing perfect white teeth. 'Aimee says you want to see me.'

Aimee had been hovering behind him but, catching Maggie's eye, she said, 'Would you like some tea, Maggie?'

'That would be nice, thanks, Aimee.'

'Well, I'll leave you two…' said Aimee uncertainly.

'Oh, it's all right,' said Maggie. 'You can listen to this, too, Aimee. I only want to ask Denis if he would be prepared to set off the fireworks at our bonfire party.'

'Is that all?' Denis grinned. 'I was beginning to wonder what all this was about.'

'Well, having a member of the fire brigade in our midst, it seemed like the obvious solution. You will do it for us, won't you, Denis?'

'Where is this party?' asked Denis, half turning to Aimee. It was true, Maggie thought, he really was handsome with his fair hair, fireman's physique and blue eyes.

'It's at Maggie's—at Mill House,' Aimee replied. 'I was going to tell you about it. We're all invited.'

'Well, we'll have to see what we can do, then, won't we?' Denis smiled again. 'Now, love, are you going to see about that cup of tea?'

'Yes, of course.' Aimee hurried away to the kitchen.

'Were you gardening when I arrived?' asked Maggie.

'Yes, I'm building a water feature, actually,' Denis replied.

'Oh, may I see?' asked Maggie. 'I love water features.'

'Of course. Come on through.' He led the way through the hall and into the kitchen. They passed a living room where Maggie caught a glimpse of Melanie bent over a table, surrounded by her school books.

In the garden Joshua and his younger brother Ben were playing on the concrete path with some toy cars. They both looked up as Maggie followed their father out of the house.

'Hello, Josh. Hello, Ben.'

'Say hello to Dr Hudson,' said Denis. Both boys seemed to have been struck dumb by the unexpected appearance of their doctor in the back garden in the middle of a Sunday afternoon.

'Hello,' Josh mumbled at last, but Ben just hung his head.

Maggie followed Denis to the far corner of the garden where he was constructing a waterfall, which would tumble over a series of large chunks of stone into a pond.

'This is very impressive,' she said as she stood back, admiring his handiwork.

'It's something I've always wanted to do,' he replied. 'We haven't had the pond for long. Couldn't have one when the kids were small, but now they're older it's not a problem.'

After Maggie had admired the fish and the rest of the garden they made their way back to the house where Aimee had brewed the tea. 'How are you getting on at school, Josh?' asked Maggie as they passed the two boys, who were still playing with their cars.

'All right,' said Josh, without looking up.

'You'll come to our bonfire party, won't you?' she went on.

He did look up at that.

'William would like you to come,' Maggie went on. 'It'll be at our house. There'll be lots to eat and a big bonfire, and we hope your dad is going to set off the fireworks for us.'

'Can I come?' asked Ben solemnly.

'Of course you can,' said Maggie with a laugh. 'You can all come. Melanie, too—Jessica will be there.'

'Melanie doesn't like Jessica,' said Josh.

'Oh, really?' For a moment Maggie was taken aback. Her daughter was usually popular amongst her classmates. 'Well, never mind. Perhaps she'll come anyway.'

They sat outside and drank their tea at a white barbecue

table. 'Isn't it amazing that we can still do this when we're right at the end of October?' Maggie lifted her face to the warmth of the afternoon sun.

'It'll certainly shorten the winter,' observed Denis.

'So, will you come to the party and do the honours?' she asked at last.

'Yes, of course.' Denis nodded.

'Thank you, Denis, you're a star.' Maggie smiled then stood up. 'I could sit here for the rest of the afternoon but I have other calls to make. Bye, boys. Thanks for tea, Aimee. Oh, by the way, how's the arm?'

'Fine,' said Aimee.

'Really?' asked Maggie searchingly.

'Yes, really.'

'Work not been too much for you?'

'You've been all right, haven't you, love?' Denis put his arm round Aimee's shoulders as she also rose to her feet.

'Yes, fine,' she said again.

They both walked to the front door with Maggie, and as they passed the living room she noticed that Melanie was no longer there.

Moments later, after a wave from the couple in the doorway, she was driving away from the house.

She carried out a further two house calls, one emergency and one routine, and was on her way home when on a sudden impulse she decided to call on Sam and tell him about her unannounced visit to the Barnes household.

Sam's house, not unlike her own, was a little off the beaten track. It was a large stone house at least a hundred years old, which had at one time been used to house a community of monks whilst their monastery had been rebuilt. There was still evidence of that early ecclesiastical influence in the first-floor casement windows with their stained-glass panels and the painted icons in the wood panelling on the staircase.

It had been Claire in the first place who'd urged Sam to buy the place when in actual fact it had been way beyond their means, but over the years it had been Sam who had come to love the house whilst Claire had found it gloomy. Maggie thought it was a wonderful house, full of atmosphere and character with its many nooks and crannies and not in the least gloomy. It was much too large for Sam now that he was on his own, they all knew that, but somehow, in spite of talk from time to time of him selling up and finding somewhere more suitable, nothing ever happened and Sam stayed where he was at St Rhadagund's.

There was a car parked outside the front door, a white VW Golf which looked vaguely familiar, but for the moment Maggie was unable to think whose it was. She found herself hesitating. If Sam had company, the last thing she wanted was to disturb him on his day off with what really was a work-related matter.

It was while she was wondering whether it wouldn't be simpler to just turn around and drive away when the front door suddenly opened and Sam emerged together with Fiona. No doubt, the practice manager had also been bothering Sam with surgery business on his day off. He saw Maggie immediately and came across to her car. 'Maggie, hello. This is a nice surprise.'

'Sam.' She spoke to him through the open car window. 'Sorry—you're busy. Would you like me to go?'

'No, don't go. Fiona is just leaving.'

'Well, if you're sure.' She opened the car door and climbed out. 'Hello, Fiona.'

'Maggie.' Fiona nodded.

'Have you been busy?' asked Sam.

'Hasn't been too bad,' Maggie replied.

'Well, I must go. Things to do.' Fiona turned and together with Sam walked to her car. Maggie frowned as she watched her. There seemed to be coolness about her today but she was at a loss to think why that should be. As Fiona drove away Sam walked back to join her and together they turned towards the house. Maggie expected him to say why the practice manager had been visiting him on a Sunday afternoon but he didn't. Instead, as they entered the spacious wood-panelled hallway of his home he said, 'I'll put the kettle on.'

'I'll be awash with tea at this rate,' said Maggie with a laugh. 'I've just come from the Barneses' place and Aimee poured huge mugs of the stuff.'

'We could have something a little stronger if you like,' Sam replied.

'Heavens, isn't it a bit early for that?'

'Probably, but I opened a rather good bottle of French red at lunchtime.'

'All right, then—I don't need too much persuading. But only one, mind—I'm still on call and I am driving.' Maggie followed him through to the kitchen where he took two glasses from a cupboard and poured the red wine.

Sam handed her one of the glasses then lifted the other. 'Cheers!' he said.

'Yes, cheers!' She took a sip before sitting down at the kitchen table.

'So what were you doing at the Barneses' place?' Sam asked, taking the chair opposite her.

'I found myself doing a house call just a stone's throw from where they live, so I decided to call in to ask Denis Barnes if he would set off the fireworks at the party.'

'And?'

'He seemed only too pleased to oblige.'

'Did you see Joshua?' asked Sam.

'Yes, I did. He was playing with his little brother in the garden. Denis himself was working on a waterfall that he's building, Melanie was doing her homework and Aimee... Well, I guess Aimee was doing what all us working mums do on a Sunday afternoon—trying to catch up with all that has to be done before Monday morning.'

'Did you get any clue as to what might be wrong?'

Maggie shook her head. 'None at all. They just seemed like a normal happy little family. Like I said before, I really do wonder if Nigel has been misinformed.'

'Let's hope so.'

'There was only one thing I found disturbing,' Maggie added after a moment.

'And what was that?'

'It was when I was talking to Josh and Ben about coming to the party. They seemed keen to come but when I happened to say that Melanie could come and that Jessica would be there, Josh looked up and said that Melanie didn't like Jessica.'

'Well, you know what kids are.' Sam shrugged. 'Friends one minute and sworn enemies the next.'

'Hmm, yes, I know. Still, I guess none of us likes to hear that a child doesn't like one of our own.'

'I wouldn't give it another thought,' said Sam firmly. 'It's like I say—just kids.'

'You're probably right.'

They sat on for a while in companionable silence, totally at ease with each other. It was Sam who broke the silence.

'So you're all set, then, for this party?' he said, swirling the contents of his glass.

'Oh, yes. I think so. Ingrid is going to town with the

cooking. I doubt if I would have even attempted it without her, but you know what she's like.'

'She really is a treasure, isn't she?'

'Absolutely. Heaven knows what I'd do if ever she wanted to move on.'

'Do you think that's likely?' Sam frowned.

'Who knows? I'm sure some man will come along one day and see what a wonderful wife she would make and whisk her away.'

'Probably best not to even contemplate that unless it actually happens,' Sam replied.

'Have you mentioned the party to Claire yet?'

'Claire?' He looked startled. 'Why would I want to mention it to her?'

'Only so that Richard and Emma will be able to come,' said Maggie hastily. 'I wasn't considering inviting Claire and Luke.'

'Thank heavens for that. You had me worried for a moment. No, I haven't said anything to Claire directly but I've told Emma about it and she was going to tell Richard and her mother.'

'Just as long as Claire doesn't throw a wobbly at the last moment and do something to prevent them from coming.'

Sam pulled a face. They both knew that was entirely possible with Claire who could be unpredictable over these things.

At last, reluctantly, Maggie stood up. 'I must go,' she said. 'I come off call at six but Ingrid is going over to see her mother so I need to get back to be with the children.'

He walked to the car with her, holding the door open, but before she got in there was a brief moment when it seemed that momentarily neither of them knew quite what to say or do next. It was a ridiculous situation as she and Sam took their leave of each other several times each day without any awkwardness, so whatever it was that made a difference that day was hard to define. Maybe it was the new awareness that had grown between them lately, which seemed to hang unspoken in the air. Maggie wasn't sure, but whatever it was it caused her to hesitate, her hand on the door, and Sam to linger, his own hand only inches from her own. But then it was over and she was inside her car, had started the engine and with a wave of her hand was away.

She glanced in her mirror once and saw that he was standing there in the middle of the drive, watching her.

Maggie blinked and peered at the road ahead. It was twilight, that elusive time between daylight and darkness when driving could be hazardous, when shadows could be indistinguishable and lights could dazzle.

She was tired after a demanding day on call and it was with a decided sense of relief when the lights of Mill House came into view and she drove down the bumpy track to her home. She pulled up on the drive to be greeted by the dogs—Galaxy, who lumbered forward thumping her tail, and Rex, barking ecstatically. After patting the Labrador and fondling the spaniel's ears, Maggie pulled her case from the car and made her way round to the kitchen door.

'Hi,' she called as she opened the door, 'I'm home!'

Ingrid was standing at the kitchen table, folding a pile of clean laundry. 'Well, that's your Sunday on call over for a few weeks,' she said, looking up as Maggie came in, shutting the door behind her.

'Yes, thank goodness,' said Maggie with a sigh. 'Where are the children?' She looked round surprised that all seemed so quiet.

'William's in the sitting room, watching a video, and Jessica's in her room. I've put this lot through the tumble-dryer.' Ingrid indicated the clothes. 'I'll iron them tomorrow. There's a lasagne in the fridge for supper. It only needs heating through.'

'Thank you, Ingrid. You're a gem, you know. But, listen, you go now—you want to see your mother, don't you?'

Ingrid nodded. 'Yes, I thought I would—so if there's nothing else I'll get along.'

While Ingrid hurried up to her room Maggie made her way into the sitting room where she found William lying full length on the carpet, watching a film.

'Hello, darling,' she said.

'Hi, Mum,' he replied, without looking up. 'This is brill.'

'Good. Well, you enjoy it. I'll just go and see Jessica.'

'She's in a mood,' said William darkly.

'Oh, dear,' said Maggie with a sigh. 'I wonder what it is this time.'

She found her daughter in her bedroom in floods of tears because her art homework wouldn't go right.

'Look at it!' she wailed. 'It's an absolute mess.'

'Let me see.' Maggie drew the large sheet of paper towards her and saw that Jessica had been trying to create an autumn collage. 'Actually,' she said after studying it, 'I think it's rather good.'

'You're just saying that,' sniffed Jessica.

'No, really. I love these leaves and the clusters of berries, but why don't you move that tree bark down to the bottom of the picture? It looks a bit off balance in the middle. And then the shells could go there—they're so delicate. What do you think?'

'I s'ppose I could try it,' said Jessica, rubbing her nose with a soggy tissue. 'It might be better.'

'Have another go, then it'll nearly be time for supper.'

As Maggie left her daughter's bedroom she reflected on the moods Jessica seemed to have suffered in the last year. There was little doubt in her mind that they were as a direct result of losing her father, for previous to his death she'd been such a happy, sunny-natured child. But her grief had generated a great deal of anger which Maggie knew had to be worked through and dealt with. She, too, had experienced intense feelings of anger at losing David and she could identify with her daughter's frustration, but in spite of that, sometimes in the process, she wondered if she hadn't been a little too lenient with her.

Later, when they all sat round the kitchen table and ate the delicious lasagne that Ingrid had prepared for them, Maggie quite casually brought up the subject of the bonfire party.

'I called in to see the Barnes family today,' she said. 'I took your suggestion, William, and asked Mr Barnes if he would set off the fireworks. He would have been coming to the party anyway with his family, and as he's a member of the fire brigade…'

'Will he bring the fire engine?' asked William hopefully.

'Of course he won't, dummy,' said Jessica.

'Jessica,' said Maggie warningly.

'Well, honestly…as if he would.' Jessica paused. 'Will they all be coming?' she asked.

'All who?' Maggie frowned.

'The Barnes family.'

'Yes. At least, I hope so. I've certainly asked them all. Why? Do you have a problem with that?'

'I don't. I like Josh,' said William, cramming more lasagne into his mouth so that his cheeks bulged.

'Don't do that, it's disgusting,' said Jessica. 'Can't you stop him, Mum?'

'William,' said Maggie firmly, 'don't put so much food in your mouth.' She turned to Jessica. 'Well? Do you have a problem with the Barnes family coming?'

'Not really.' Jessica pulled a face and shrugged.

'You get on with Melanie, don't you?'

'Well…not exactly.'

'What do you mean, "not exactly"?' Maggie spoke more sharply than she'd intended, and Jessica threw her a sullen look.

'No one does,' she muttered. 'Honestly, Mum, she's so weird… No one really likes her…'

'Are you trying to tell me that you all gang up on the poor girl?' demanded Maggie. Suddenly all she could see was Josh's face when he'd said that Melanie didn't like Jessica.

'No, we don't actually gang up on her…' Jessica looked wary now and even William had stopped eating and was looking from his mother to his sister as the conversation between them looked as if it might be about to escalate into something interesting.

'I hope there's no bullying, Jessica,' said Maggie. 'Because if there is…' She didn't finish the sentence but the threat was carried in the tone of her voice.

'I'm not a bully!' declared Jessica hotly, her face growing red.

'Bullying can take many forms,' Maggie replied crisply. 'So tell me, how is Melanie treated by the girls in your form?'

'Sometimes we laugh at her—but she *is* odd, Mum, she really is.' Jessica hastened to defend the actions of herself and her friends but, catching sight of Maggie's expression, she went on hurriedly, 'But mostly we just leave her alone.'

'Excluding someone from your circle can be one of the worst forms of bullying,' said Maggie crisply. 'I'm disappointed in you, Jessica. I expected better from you. In future I want you to make a special effort where Melanie is concerned. I want you to include her in the things you do and you can start by telling her how pleased you are that she's coming to the party.'

'But *Mum*!' wailed Jessica.

'That's enough, Jessica,' said Maggie firmly. 'I don't want to hear another word. Now, William, would you like some rhubarb crumble?'

'Yes, please!' William, his eyes shining, sighed ecstatically.

With that the subject of the Barnes family was effectively closed, but later, when the children were in bed and she herself was just drifting off to sleep, Maggie found herself thinking of her conversation with Jessica and wondering just what it was about Melanie that made the other children in her class think of her as being odd. But her very last thought before sleep claimed her was of her visit to Sam and of that strange moment of indecisiveness between them when she had gone to get into her car. Maybe she should simply have given Sam a kiss on the cheek, not that they could do that each day at the surgery—she smiled at the very thought—but maybe when they were alone it wouldn't matter and it would certainly prevent any such moment of awkwardness again.

CHAPTER EIGHT

'THAT looks nasty—how did you do it?' Sam lifted the man's hand and carefully investigated the long splinter of wood that was firmly embedded in the fleshy area on the outer edge.

'I was helping my son-in-law make some shelves for his kitchen. It happened so quickly…'

'Most accidents do,' Sam replied. 'I'd like you to come along to the treatment room with me so I can remove it. Then we'll check if your antitetanus is up to date and I'll ask the nurse to dress this for you.' As he finished speaking he led the way out of his consulting room and down the stairs to the treatment room.

He tapped on the door and on entering found that Dawn had just completed syringing a patient's ears.

'Oh, Dawn,' he said in surprise, 'it's you. I thought Aimee was on duty this morning.'

'She phoned in sick,' Dawn replied.

'I see. Well, this is Gordon Jackman,' Sam explained. 'He's got rather a vicious-looking splinter in his hand. I need to remove it for him.'

Dawn's patient left the treatment room and while she checked Gordon Jackman's antitetanus record chart on the computer Sam drew up a shot of local anaesthetic to deaden the pain.

'The splinter has gone in at quite an angle,' he explained as he administered the injection. 'This will enable me to dig around a bit without you hitting the roof.'

'I don't think I'll watch,' Gordon replied.

'Bit squeamish, are you?' asked Sam with a chuckle.

'I've never liked the sight of blood. Not like my wife. She loves all those hospital programmes on the telly—the gorier the better.'

Sam found he had to make a small incision in order to grasp the end of the splinter with a pair of tweezers. Gently but firmly he began to pull. The splinter began to move then… 'Damn!' he muttered under his breath.

'What is it?' asked Gordon Jackman anxiously.

'It's broken,' Sam replied. 'That's just what I didn't want to happen. Not to worry,' he added cheerfully. 'I'll just have to carry out a repeat performance a little lower down, that's all.'

He made a second incision but the lower end of the splinter was even more deeply embedded and it took him some considerable time to locate the end and then grasp it with the tweezers. And even when he did so he was unable to draw out the remaining portion of wood.

'It doesn't want to move,' he said.

'What happens if it won't come out?' asked Gordon.

'We may have to send you to Casualty,' Sam replied.

'Oh, no!'

'They're more able to cope with this sort of thing than we are here,' Sam explained.

'Well, keep trying, Dr Neville. I don't like hospitals.'

'Right, let's have another go.' Sam looked up. 'Dawn could you shift that light over here, please?'

Dawn obliged and moved the light so that it shone directly onto the patient's hand.

'That's better, thanks.'

Sam began to probe again into the soft fleshy area. This time he couldn't even see the tip of the splinter, which seemed to have become obscured by blood, but just as he was on the point of giving up he saw the small dark tip protruding slightly from the raw flesh. 'Ah,' he said significantly. 'There it is. Now, if I can just get hold of it again... Yes, that's it.' With the tweezers he gripped the tiny piece of wood and began to pull, hoping as he did so that it wouldn't break again. If it did he knew he would have no chance at all of withdrawing the last remaining fragment.

Slowly but surely the remainder of the splinter began to move until at last with a grunt of satisfaction Sam withdrew it all from Gordon's hand. Carefully he placed the splinter onto a gauze pad and showed it to the patient. 'There you are,' he said. 'Here's the offending object.'

'It was a fair old size, wasn't it?' said Gordon in awe. 'Well, thanks, Dr Neville. Thank you very much.'

'I think I'd like to put a couple of Steri-Strips over the wound,' said Sam. With a pad of gauze, which Dawn passed to him, he staunched the flow of blood. 'After that Sister Prentice will dress this for you. All right, Sister?' He turned to Dawn who passed him a packet of Steri-Strips.

'Yes, of course, and I'll also give an antitetanus booster just to be on the safe side.' As Sam administered the Steri-Strips she went on, 'Are you all right, Mr Jackman? You're looking a little pale.'

'Yes, I'm OK.' Gordon nodded. 'But I don't think I'll be putting up any more shelves today.'

After Dawn had given the injection and Gordon had left the treatment room, Sam, who was washing his hands in the basin, turned to Dawn. 'Do we know what's wrong with Aimee?' he asked.

'Fiona said a migraine,' Dawn replied as she set about clearing up the gauze, swabs and empty packets.

'Does she normally suffer from migraine?' asked Sam.

'Not that I know of.' Dawn shook her head. 'I must

admit I was quite surprised when Fiona phoned and asked if I could come in and cover for Aimee.'

'Has her arm been playing her up since she came back to work?'

'I don't think so. But, having said that, I don't really work alongside Aimee so probably I'm not the best person to ask.'

'Hmm, right.' Sam wiped his hands with a paper towel then, rolling it into a ball, sent it with deadly accuracy into the waste bin. 'Don't forget the staff meeting later on,' he said as he headed towards the door.

'As if I could.' Dawn pulled a face. 'It was the first thing Fiona reminded me of when I arrived this morning.'

Maggie glanced at her watch. She had one more house call to make. If she was quick she could do that and still be back at the centre for the staff meeting. She was sitting in her car in the high street, having just popped into the bank after visiting an elderly gentleman who was recovering from a recent stroke. It had been raining heavily. Large puddles filled the gutters and as the first sunshine of the day struggled through the grey clouds the wet road shone so brightly it made Maggie's eyes ache. She was about to start the engine when suddenly someone tapped on the window. Looking up, she saw Rory Scott in waxed jacket and checked cap peering into the car. She immediately wound down the window. 'Rory, hello. How are you?'

'Maggie. I'm fine, thanks, and yourself?'

'Yes. I don't like all this wet weather. Tell me, how is Alison?'

'She's pretty good…'

'No more bleeding?'

'No.'

'I hope she's still taking it easy.'

'Er, yes…'

'Is there anything wrong, Rory?' Maggie frowned.

'Well, I know you told her to rest and she has, but the thing is, Maggie, even now that the danger has passed she seems reluctant to leave the bedroom. You did say it was all right for her to resume a reasonably normal life, didn't you?'

'Yes, I did. But I know women can become terribly anxious in these circumstances.' She paused. 'I was going to say I'll pop over and see her, but on second thoughts I think it might be better if you could persuade her to come into the surgery and see me. Look, why don't you drop in this afternoon about two o'clock and I'll see her before my surgery? Could you do that, Rory?'

A doubtful look spread across his face. 'I'll do my best but she really does seem to have got it into her head that the slightest exertion will result in her losing the baby.'

'Well, see what you can do, but if she gets really upset let me know and I'll come and talk to her.'

After saying goodbye to Rory, Maggie drove out of the high street and on to her final house call of the day—a young man with motor neurone disease who was becoming increasingly incapacitated. His young wife and the dedicated team of community nurses were nursing him at home. The prognosis wasn't good and he was in great pain and discomfort, but whenever Maggie visited, in spite of the fact that the situation reminded her of how David had been when he'd been so ill, she found herself spiritually uplifted by the love, laughter and sheer optimism that surrounded him. It was a humbling experience and she always left the house in a quiet and reflective frame of mind.

On that particular morning, by the time she got back to

the surgery it was to find that the staff meeting had already started.

'Only just.' Holly, who was on duty in Reception, responded to her query. 'I was to ask you to go up as soon as you arrived.'

'Who asked you to do that?' Maggie was faintly surprised. It didn't sound the sort of thing that either Sam or Jon would have said.

'Fiona,' said Holly.

'Oh. Oh, I see,' said Maggie. 'Well, I suppose I'd better go up then and not keep them waiting any longer.' She was about to walk towards the stairs when Holly stopped her.

'Dr Hudson, do you think they'll be sorting out the new filing system at this meeting?'

'Yes, I think that was one of the things on the agenda.'

'Thank goodness for that,' said Holly, rolling her eyes.

'Why, what's wrong?'

'It's driving me mad,' said Holly. 'Only don't say I said so, will you? It's just that Jackie is still doing it her way and Fiona is insisting that we all adopt her new method. Katie and I don't know where we are. We were only saying this morning that we don't think we can put up with much more of it. We were thinking of going down to the job centre to see what else is going.'

'Oh, don't say that, Holly,' said Maggie in alarm. The thought of losing two receptionists in one fell swoop was more than she could contemplate at the end of a busy morning.

'Something will have to be done.' Holly had apparently got into her stride now after her initial timidity.

'I'll see what I can do,' promised Maggie. 'Don't worry about it.'

Leaving Reception, she hurried up the stairs and along

the corridor to the staffroom. The room was full and the meeting had indeed started.

'I'm sorry I'm late.' Maggie swept the assembled staff with her glance but her apology was directed towards Sam.

Sam looked up and as his gaze met hers Maggie unexpectedly felt her heart turn over. 'That's all right, Maggie,' he said. 'We've only just started. There's a seat over here. We were just discussing the possibility of updating the appointments system.'

'As well as the filing system?' Maggie, in a desperate attempt to pull herself together, spoke without thinking.

'Fiona seems to think it necessary,' Sam replied.

'The system is antiquated,' said Fiona coolly. 'Likewise the filing system. We're in the twenty-first century now in case no one had noticed. In my last practice these new systems were in place and up and running a couple of years ago.'

Maggie shot a surreptitious glance in Jackie's direction and got the distinct impression that the senior receptionist only just bit back a retort to the effect that if that was the case and Fiona's old practice had been so perfect maybe she should have stayed there.

'If you don't move with the times there'll be trouble,' Fiona said flatly.

Maggie wanted to ask her what sort of trouble she had in mind but somehow she couldn't quite bring herself to do so. Instead she said, 'About the filing system, Fiona— I know that before you came Jackie and the other girls put a lot of time into updating our present system and I have to say it seemed to be working well.' As she finished speaking she was aware of a grateful look from Jackie.

'It's old-fashioned,' said Fiona with a sigh. 'I'm sorry, but it just is.'

'Does that actually matter if it works?' asked Dawn.

Fiona took a deep breath. 'When you appointed me as practice manager I understood that I would have carte blanche to streamline the running of the administrative side of this practice.'

'Fiona, I'm sure no one wants to prevent you from improving the efficiency of the practice.' It was Sam who answered, Sam who, as senior partner, found himself in the role of peacemaker. 'Maybe it would help if you and Jackie worked together over these matters rather than against each other.' Hopefully he glanced from Fiona to Jackie. 'Then, when things are worked out, Jackie can instruct the other girls.'

'We're the ones who'll need instruction,' said Jon with a wry grin.

'Well, yes. Quite.' Sam nodded in rueful agreement. 'Now, can we press on with other matters?' He glanced round at the others. 'Next on the agenda is cover for staff holidays.'

A groan rippled round the room. Maggie felt sorry for Sam knowing as she did how little he'd wanted to take on the role of senior partner.

The meeting wore on, with one topic after another being discussed, some being solved and others deferred, until at last Sam brought the meeting to a close and the members of staff began filing out of the staffroom.

'Maggie.' Fiona paused as she passed her. 'Could I come and see you after your afternoon surgery?'

'Yes, of course.' As Fiona left the room Maggie turned and found that she, Sam and Jon were the only ones left.

'Well, I'm glad that's over,' said Sam with a sigh.

'I thought you handled things very well,' said Maggie.

'Did you?' Sam frowned doubtfully. 'All this in-house wrangling really isn't my cup of tea.'

'Maybe you were right in the first place about us not needing a practice manager,' said Maggie thoughtfully.

'I think we've just got to give Fiona a chance,' said Jon. 'Her ideas—well, some of them at least—are very good, but implementing them in this practice is another matter.'

'You can say that again.' Maggie pulled a face. 'I thought if we had a practice manager it would bring about better liaison with the staff, but ever since Fiona arrived we seem to have had nothing but bickering. And when I spoke to Holly this morning it sounded as if she and Katie might well be on the point of looking for other jobs.'

Sam looked startled. 'As bad as that?'

'I'd hate to lose either of them. Good receptionists are hard to come by. And no matter how good Fiona is, we don't want the rest of the staff walking out.'

'Absolutely not,' said Sam.

'True,' Jon agreed. 'But I doubt it'll come to that—and you have to admit, Sam, Fiona has brightened the place up a bit. It's amazing what a pretty face and a pair of long legs will do to boost morale.'

'Honestly, you men!' Maggie gave an exasperated sigh as with a wink and a grin Jon scooped up his bag and hurried out of the room. She was about to follow him when Sam called her back.

'Maggie, did you know Aimee was off sick again?'

'No, I didn't.' She paused and stared at him. 'What's wrong, do you know?'

'Dawn said a migraine.'

'I've never known Aimee to suffer from migraine before.'

'That's what I thought,' said Sam.

'Maybe I'll give her a ring later when I get a minute.'

Maggie only had time for a quick sandwich and a coffee, which she took in her consulting room whilst catching up on paperwork, before Holly buzzed through to say that Alison Scott was in Reception with her husband, Rory.

'Send them up, please, Holly,' said Maggie, taking the last mouthful of her coffee.

Alison looked pale, tired and tearful when a few minutes later she and Rory came into Maggie's consulting room.

'Alison, come in and sit down,' Maggie greeted her after a quick, significant glance at Rory. 'Now, tell me, how have you been?'

'Tired,' Alison admitted. 'And, well, scared I suppose.'

'Scared?'

'Yes. Scared that the same thing is going to happen again.'

'That's understandable, Alison,' said Maggie gently, 'but it does seem as if everything has settled down again. I would, however, like to examine you and just check your blood pressure.'

Maggie carried out her examination and then found Alison's blood pressure to be normal. 'When is your next hospital check-up due?' she asked as Alison rearranged her clothing.

'Next week.' It was Rory who answered.

'I want you to carry on taking things easy until after that check-up,' said Maggie. 'By that, I mean no heavy housework and continuing to have a rest on the bed after lunch each day. After that, we'll review things again.'

'What about going out, Maggie?' asked Rory.

'There's no reason why you shouldn't go out, Alison. Light exercise is good for you—just be careful not to overtire yourself.' Maggie paused then thoughtfully she went on, 'Listen, we're having a bonfire party on the fifth—why don't you both come?'

'I don't know...' Alison looked doubtful.

'Go on, it'll be fun. It's at Mill House, it won't be late and if you feel tired you can always go indoors and rest. What do you say?'

'Well, if you think it will be all right...'

'Thanks, Maggie,' said Rory. 'We'd love to come.'

After Alison and Rory had left Maggie started her surgery and worked steadily through the list of patients for the next couple of hours. By the time Holly informed her that she had just seen her last patient she was beginning to flag and the thought of home, the children, the fireside and Ingrid's cooking was becoming more attractive by the minute. She wondered what Sam was doing and was on the point of ringing through to his room to ask him if he'd like to join them for supper when there came a tap on her door.

'Come in,' she called wearily. 'Oh, Fiona, it's you.' She'd forgotten she'd agreed to see the practice manager at the end of her surgery and her heart sank at the prospect of yet more discussion over practice matters.

'You did say...' Fiona began as she came right into the room.

'Yes, of course. Come in and sit down. What can I do for you? Is it more problems with the staff?'

'No, actually, not that.' Fiona gave a tight little smile. 'This time it's for me.'

'How may I help? Are you feeling unwell?' Maggie looked closely at the young woman on the other side of the desk. She certainly didn't look unwell. In fact, if anything, she looked the picture of health.

'No, I'm fine. Never felt better. Why I wanted to see you was to ask you to prescribe the Pill for me.'

Maggie frowned. 'The last time we discussed this you told me you'd stopped taking the Pill and were happy to give your body a rest.'

'Yes. I know.' Fiona nodded. 'But that was mainly because I wasn't in a relationship then.'

'So are you saying that now you are?'

'Well, let's just say I could be. I've met someone and things look as if they could be heading in that direction. Oh, don't worry, I'm well aware of practising safe sex but I don't want to take any chances in the pregnancy stakes either.'

'Can I assume this person isn't the same one you were involved with before?' asked Maggie as she pressed the keys on her keyboard to bring Fiona's medical chart to her computer screen.

'Yes. That relationship died some time ago. This is someone new. It's very exciting and I hope—no, I think I can go as far as to say I'm certain—it's going places. You know when something's right, don't you? When the chemistry is there and the magic is working?'

'Yes, I suppose you do.' Maggie suddenly recalled the moment earlier in the day when Sam's eyes had met hers and she'd felt her heart turn over. 'I do know what you mean.' She paused. 'Now, let's see, presumably the last brand of Pill you were taking suited you. Are you happy to go back onto that brand again?'

'Oh, yes,' Fiona replied. 'I felt very well whilst I was taking it.'

'Good. Let me check your blood pressure.'

A few minutes later Maggie removed the cuff from Fiona's arm. 'That's fine,' she said, draping her stethoscope around her neck. 'When did you have your last smear?'

'I'm not sure offhand. I'd have to check. But I think I'm probably due for one.'

'In that case, ask Aimee or Dawn to fit you in on one of my smear clinics.' Turning back to her computer, Maggie pressed the print button and as the prescription began to print out, she said, 'This new man in your life— is it anyone we know?' When Fiona didn't reply she threw her a quick glance.

'Actually…' Fiona allowed her gaze briefly to meet Maggie's '…if you don't mind, I'd rather not say. It really is very early days as yet and I don't want to tempt fate by talking about it if it isn't going to happen after all—if you get my meaning.'

'I know exactly what you mean. Something to do with not counting chickens.' Maggie tore off the prescription and handed it to Fiona. 'Well, I wish you all the best anyway.'

'Thanks, Maggie.' Fiona stood up. 'I think I'm going to call it a day. Have you finished?'

'Just about. Can't say I'm sorry either. It's been one of those days.'

'Well, I'll see you in the morning. Night, Maggie.'

'Goodnight, Fiona.' She watched as the practice manager left the room. She certainly did look happy, there was no doubt about that, and Maggie found herself wondering who the new man in her life was. It was pretty obvious it was someone they knew if Fiona's reluctance to reveal his identity was anything to go by. Idly she wondered if it could be Jon. After all, it was a well-known fact that he found it impossible to resist a pretty face and a new one on the scene at that, and he had been the one to stick up for Fiona over the staff issues as if he feared that if things got too bad she might leave.

By the time she left her consulting room it was to find

that Sam had already left the surgery. It had been her intention to ask him over to Mill House to supper but there was no sign of him, either in the building or the car park and when she tried his mobile it was to find it was switched off.

It was with a vague sense of disappointment that Maggie drove home. She'd been looking forward to seeing Sam that evening. There were things she wanted to discuss with him—practice matters and the plans for the forthcoming bonfire party which seemed to be looming up at a rapidly alarming rate. But quite apart from that, and without analysing the reason too deeply, she knew she simply wanted to be with him.

It was quite late that same evening, after the children were in bed, that Maggie remembered she hadn't phoned Aimee. She was annoyed with herself for having forgotten but she decided that it was too late to bother the Barnes household. If Aimee had indeed had a migraine, hopefully she would be asleep by now and the last thing she would want would be to talk to her boss, even if her boss did also happen to be her doctor. Tomorrow would be quite soon enough. Instead, she tried Sam again but his mobile was still switched off and when she tried his home number it was switched through to the answering machine.

With the same sense of disappointment she'd felt earlier, she hung up. Turning out her light, she attempted to go to sleep.

CHAPTER NINE

MAGGIE didn't have to phone Aimee as it happened because the following day the practice nurse was back on duty. When Maggie rushed into the treatment room to restock her bag with dressing packs Aimee was right there, carrying out a stock check.

'Aimee!' Maggie exclaimed. 'There you are. I was going to phone you this morning. Are you all right?'

'Yes,' said Aimee quickly. 'Yes, I'm fine, thanks.'

'You don't look fine.' Maggie peered at her and was concerned to see that she looked tired and drawn.

'I'm OK. Really I am. It was only a migraine, that's all.'

'But you've not been troubled by migraine before, have you?'

'Er, no.' Aimee looked a bit flustered and Maggie found herself wondering if she'd simply taken a day off work for some other reason and was covering up.

'Aimee, if you ever want to have a chat with me about it sometime, you know I'm here.' she said.

'Yes. All right. Thanks Maggie.' Aimee went back to her stock lists while Maggie collected the dressing packs and returned to her consulting room.

She took off her jacket and hung it behind the door, but as she passed the window to reach her desk a movement in the car park below caught her eye and she paused and looked down. Jon had just got out of his car and was talking to Fiona. Their heads were close together as if the nature of their conversation was confidential—or per-

sonal—and even as Maggie watched, Fiona looked up into
Jon's face and laughed. He looked down at her but because he had his back to the building Maggie couldn't see
his expression. Briefly Fiona laid her hand on his arm and,
leaning towards him, said something, which from her
body language was obviously meant for his ears alone.
Then they drew apart and, passing from Maggie's view,
entered the building together.

Maggie smiled. It looked as if she'd been right and Jon
was indeed the new man in Fiona's life. Well, if that was
the case she was glad for them—she liked it when two
people found happiness with each other.

And that happiness seemed to be echoing a chord somewhere within herself for as the autumn days had shortened
she'd found herself being drawn more and more towards
Sam and looking at him in an entirely new light. He had
been her dearest friend for so long but this was something
new, something different, something exciting. This meeting of glances when either of them entered a room where
the other was and this heightened sense of awareness
which Maggie was sure Sam also was experiencing whenever they were together. No word had as yet been spoken
between them but for the time being Maggie was content
simply to let the feeling grow.

The days before the fifth of November saw much wet and
wild weather, with gales roaring up through the channel
and gusts of up to ninety miles an hour hitting the
Needles. The children fretted that the party wouldn't be
able to take place but Ingrid had cleverly stored old junk
for the bonfire in the garage to prevent it getting wet while
indoors she carried on with her baking, freezing and stor-
ing.

Sam called several times at Mill House and amidst

much secrecy and hilarity he and the children disappeared to the summerhouse at the bottom of the garden to work on the Guy they were making. It was a secret even from Maggie and Ingrid.

'It's brilliant,' said Jessica. 'You just wait until you see it.'

'It's so good of Dr Neville to help the children,' observed Ingrid, her hands in a bowl of pastry as she made yet more pies for the party.

'Yes,' Maggie agreed with a little sigh. 'He's so good with them. Wills adores him and even Jessica does more for him than she would for me.'

To everyone's relief, the morning of the fifth dawned bright and sharp and became a day where the deepest of blue skies formed a perfect backdrop for the vibrant colours of autumn.

Maggie had taken an annual leave day and spent most of it working with Ingrid, preparing for the party. After surgery, as dusk fell, Sam arrived and set up both his own and Maggie's portable barbecues in the garage. Maggie had made a huge bowl of spiced fruit punch, which she set in the centre of the kitchen table, surrounding it with salads and dips and all Ingrid's mouth-watering delicacies—the poacher's pies, the pasties and her speciality, the apple strudel topped with thick cream.

By six-thirty the first guests were beginning to arrive—Richard and Emma brought over by Luke who, Maggie thought, looked as if he wouldn't have minded staying himself and joining in the fun, Jackie and her partner Iain with their son Max, and the Barnes family who arrived in Denis's car. Sam immediately whisked Denis away to the far corner of the garden reserved for the bonfire and the fireworks while Aimee helped Maggie to dispense drinks.

The rest of the staff arrived, including Jon, Moira, Katie

and Holly, plus her current boyfriend. By this time Sam had the barbecues well under way and the delicious smoky aroma of char-grilled meat wafted into the house through the open garage doors. In the kitchen Maggie was presiding over the fruit punch when a tall, slightly stooped figure strolled into the room.

'Leonard!' she exclaimed in delight, a punch-filled cup poised in the air. 'You made it—how wonderful!'

'Maggie, darling.' Leaning across the table, he kissed her cheek. 'How could I resist one of your parties?'

Suddenly, as she stared at Leonard, the man who had helped both David and Sam to start up the practice and who, although having now retired, had remained a dear friend to them all in spite of health problems, her eyes filled with tears. Leonard must have seen her tears because quickly he spoke again. 'There's a time for everything Maggie,' he said softly, 'and it's time for the sound of laughter again in Mill House.'

'Dear Leonard, I do believe you are right as usual,' she said softly. With a smile he took a cup of punch and moved away to talk to some of the others.

There was the sound of a commotion outside in the garden, with shouts and squeals of delight, and Maggie hurried to the door, along with the others who had been crammed in the kitchen, to find that Sam, Jessica and William had been joined by Richard and Emma and were processing from the summerhouse bearing between them the figure of Guy Fawkes, resplendent in dark trousers, a striped blazer and a straw boater. The face sported a carefully drawn pencil moustache and a monocle.

'Isn't he brilliant?' cried Jessica. 'Sam gave us the clothes. We've been making him for ages—haven't we, Wills?'

'Yes, for ages!' Wills agreed.

Maggie turned to Sam in amazement. 'Wherever did you get those clothes?'

'I had them for a fancy-dress party I went to in my student days,' Sam admitted sheepishly.

'But surely you don't want to burn them!' Maggie exclaimed.

'I can't imagine I'll ever want them again. In fact, I doubt whether I'd even get into them now.' Sam grinned ruefully as between them they bore the Guy down the garden to the large patch of wasteland at the end where earlier in the day they'd all built the bonfire. Together they hoisted the figure of the Guy onto the top then Sam took himself off to the garage to tend to his barbecue. As Maggie and the children made their way back to the house, Maggie put an arm around her daughter.

'Jessica,' she said softly, 'please, ask Melanie to join you to watch the fireworks.'

'Oh, Mum, do I have to?'

'Yes, Jessica! You have to,' Maggie replied firmly. 'Remember what we said.'

'Oh, all right,' muttered Jessica. 'Where is she?'

'She was in the kitchen with her brothers the last I saw her.'

'All right. I'll go and fetch her. Mr Barnes said he's going to light the bonfire soon.' Jessica darted back indoors and Maggie hurried across to the garage where Sam was cooking the food.

Clad in jeans, a warm fleece jacket and a striped apron, he looked up as Maggie approached and his eyes lit up. She noticed a smear of charcoal on his cheek, his dark hair was ruffled and quite suddenly her throat tightened with emotion as a feeling of utter happiness flooded over her.

'Maggie.' He smiled. 'Everything OK?'

'Yes, Sam. Everything's fine. Most people have arrived, I think. Denis is about to light the bonfire. How's the cooking going?'

'It's well under way.'

'It smells delicious,' she replied with a laugh. Turning sharply, she almost collided with someone who was about to enter the garage.

'Oh, Fiona,' she said quickly. 'Sorry, I didn't see you there.'

'I thought I'd see if Sam needs a hand,' Fiona replied.

'Well, he seems to be coping very well…'

'Hello, Sam.' Fiona walked past Maggie and into the garage. She was wearing close-fitting black trousers, which she'd tucked into a pair of high black boots. With these she wore a cream poloneck chenille sweater and a padded body warmer and her long hair was coiled into a knot at the back of her head and fastened with a bow. The whole effect managed to be both fetching and appropriate for the occasion.

As Maggie slunk back to the kitchen she glanced ruefully down at the long skirt, huge sweater and Wellington boots she was wearing and wished she'd had more time to consider her own attire for the evening.

And quite suddenly, unreasonably so, she found she didn't want to leave Fiona with Sam. *She* wanted to stay with him, to help him, to be at his side when the others came for their food—which was utterly ridiculous as they'd already agreed that she should be in the house, keeping an eye on things, while Sam was outside in the garage.

She'd barely got back into the kitchen, greeted a few more people who'd just arrived, including Alison and Rory, and poured more drinks when William dashed in, clutching a hamburger in one hand, to say that Mr Barnes was lighting the bonfire and would they all, please, come outside.

Everyone poured out of the house into the garden and stood around in little groups, clutching their drinks, as Denis lit the bonfire. There was a moment's silence then a collective murmur of satisfaction as the flames took hold and flickered upwards around the large mound of wood and junk to the blazer-clad Guy Fawkes seated on the top.

After a few minutes, when the fire was crackling merrily, the first rocket soared into the air accompanied by a gasp from those watching, and with a bang and a shower of red and green stars the firework display began. Maggie found herself beside Leonard and Aimee, both of whom seemed to be enjoying the display. The fireworks were many and varied—from deafening firecrackers that exploded in blinding flashes of light to more sedate set pieces and the ever-popular rocket cascades, each one a little more spectacular than the last, bringing forth the time-honoured oohs and ahhs from those watching.

Maggie found herself looking around at the others—at the faces of the children aglow in the light from the fire as with heads tilted back and mouths open they watched the fireworks, and the adults, all people she knew well either as friends or colleagues or both. She glanced sideways at Leonard, his dear face illuminated in the firelight, at Aimee on her other side who appeared relaxed tonight. Maybe they'd been wrong about their fears for the family, Maggie certainly hoped so. The children at least seemed happy as they joined in the fun with the others.

Alison and Rory were standing just outside the kitchen door; Rory had one arm protectively around his wife while Alison herself seemed contented if a little quiet. Watching them together, it made Maggie suddenly aware of just how much she'd missed being part of a couple.

She swallowed and, turning away, looked up at the bed-room window where she could just make out the outlines of two figures. She smiled to herself. Ingrid and her mother Ellen were upstairs looking after the two dogs while the fireworks were under way, just as they'd promised they would.

She found her gaze searching for Sam. She hadn't been able to see him a moment ago and had assumed he was still in the garage, but now as she looked again she saw that he was standing on the drive, watching the display. His head was thrown back and Maggie could see that he was laughing. Once again she felt that tightening of her throat, but even as she watched him he was joined by a second figure as Fiona moved forward and, standing close beside him, slipped her hand through his arm.

Maggie frowned and looked round the garden. Where was Jon, for heaven's sake? Shouldn't he be the one Fiona was snuggling up to? She spied him at last on the far side of the garden, enjoying a drink with Jackie's partner, Iain. She turned away and began to walk into the house.

'Maggie,' said Leonard as she passed him, 'you'll miss the fireworks.'

'It's all right,' she replied quickly. 'I'm just going to check on the soup—I won't be long.'

'Do you want any help?'

'No, Leonard. You stay with Aimee.' Turning away, Maggie hurried into the house.

The two large pots of soup—one of tomato and the other of leek and potato—were simmering gently on the Aga. After checking them, Maggie watched the rest of the firework display from the kitchen doorway.

The last rockets, signifying the end of the show, soared into the night sky and, accompanied by cheering and applause, exploded into a multitude of gold and silver stars.

Turning back to the Aga, Maggie picked up the ladle and prepared to dispense the hot soup.

'Let me do that.' Ingrid was suddenly at her side. 'You mingle with your guests.'

'Were the dogs all right?' Maggie asked anxiously.

'Yes, they're fine,' Ingrid replied. 'The fireworks were wonderful, weren't they?'

'Absolutely. I think the first bowl of soup should go to Denis.'

Maggie looked up as Aimee came into the kitchen with Leonard. She was laughing at something he'd just said and Maggie found herself thinking that maybe this party was proving to be a good thing for everyone.

'Aimee,' she said, 'we were just saying that we think the first bowl of soup should go to Denis for all his hard work.'

'Did I hear my name?' Before Aimee could answer, Denis was there in the kitchen.

'Oh, Denis, there you are,' said Maggie. 'You did a marvellous job out there. Would you like some soup?'

'Is there nothing stronger?' Denis looked around. 'I feel in need of a drink after all that.'

'Yes, of course,' Maggie replied. 'There's cider, lager or…or a Scotch if you prefer.'

'A Scotch sounds more like it.' Denis glanced at Aimee, who was still standing beside Leonard. 'You'll drive home, won't you, love?'

'I usually do,' she replied quietly.

'Is the bonfire all right?' asked Maggie as she poured a whisky for Denis.

'Yes,' he replied. 'Iain's keeping an eye on it.'

Later, when everyone was happily munching their way through the food—Ingrid's delicacies, Sam's barbecued meats and Maggie's salads and dips—Maggie slipped into the sitting room to change the music. She found Emma in there.

'Emma? Whatever are you doing in here all on your own?' she said in surprise.

'Richard upset me,' said Emma with a pout.

'Oh? How did he do that?' Maggie sat beside Emma and put her arm around her.

'He said he's going to go and live with Daddy.'

'Really? And does Daddy know about this?'

'Not yet.' Emma shook her head.

'So you're upset because you don't want him to go—is that it?' asked Maggie slowly, wondering even as she said it what Sam would make of this turn of events.

'No.' Emma shook her head and her dark curls bounced. 'I was upset because he said I should want to go as well.'

'And don't you want to go?'

'I don't know. I'd like to live with Daddy, but I like living with Mummy and Luke as well. And then there's Mister Snow and I don't think Daddy would have room for Mister Snow because he doesn't have a field like Luke does…'

'Well, if I were you, Emma, I shouldn't get upset,' said Maggie. 'Wait and see what happens. It may not be prac-tical for Richard to live with your dad. After all, he's at work all day and even at weekends he's sometimes on call.'

'And at night,' said Emma nodding vigorously. 'I told Richard he wouldn't be able to stay at home on his own at night.'

'Look, I don't think you should worry about this any more. You run along and find the other children. I think I heard someone say the chestnuts that Mr Barnes roasted in the fire were ready—why don't you go and see?'

'All right.' As Emma ran from the room she almost collided with Jon in the doorway.

'Whoa there, young lady. Steady on.' He laughed as she squeezed past him then, catching sight of Maggie, he said, 'Maggie, there you are. I've someone here I'd like you to meet.' He turned and Maggie saw that by his side was a young, dark-haired woman whom she'd never seen before. 'This is Beverley,' he said, taking the woman's hand and drawing her forward. 'She's just arrived. I thought tonight would be a good opportunity for her to meet everyone. Beverley, this is my partner, Maggie Hudson.'

'Hello, Maggie.' The girl smiled. 'Sorry I'm late—I had a late meeting at work.'

'Not at all.' Maggie smiled back. 'I'm delighted to meet you. Have you known Jon for long?'

'About a month now, isn't it, darling?' Beverley turned and looked up at Jon with adoring eyes.

He smiled. 'Yes,' he replied. Looking at Maggie again, he said, 'Beverley is a partner with the new firm of solicitors in Millbury.'

'I see,' said Maggie. 'Well, enjoy the party.'

'Thanks.' Jon grinned. 'Come on, Bev, I want you to meet Sam—let's go and find him.'

Maggie watched Jon and Beverley leave the room and it was only after they'd gone that it suddenly dawned on her that if Jon had been going out with Beverley for the last month, she'd been wrong in her assumption that he was the new man in Fiona's life. Slowly she walked out of the sitting room to join the others.

It seemed in no time at all the party was over and people began to leave.

'Great party, Maggie...'

'Thank you so much...'

'You must come to us…'

In the midst of the flurry of farewells the phone rang.

'It's the on-call doctor,' said Ingrid, holding the receiver towards Maggie.

'I'll take it,' said Sam. 'I thought Mervin might need some help tonight.' He listened carefully for a while. 'All right, Mervin,' he said at last. 'Leave that one to me.'

'What is it?' asked Maggie quietly.

'It's Nadine Harrington,' Sam replied. 'Apparently she's locked herself in a bedroom after threatening suicide.'

'I'll go,' said Maggie. 'Nadine's my patient.'

'In that case,' said Sam. 'I'll come with you. It sounds as if you may be glad of some help.'

CHAPTER TEN

THEY took Sam's car and travelled through the darkness from Mill House to Bob's and Nadine's home on the far side of Millbury. They had left the children in the capable hands of Ingrid and her mother and the handful of guests who hadn't yet left the party.

'It was a great party, Sam.' Maggie leaned her head back against the headrest of Sam's car, happy to let him drive.

'It was,' he agreed. 'Everyone said so. The food was delicious—Ingrid really came up trumps.' He was silent for a moment, concentrating on the road ahead. 'What did you think of Jon's new girlfriend?' he asked after a while.

'She seemed very nice,' Maggie replied. 'But I have to say Jon's been a dark horse over this. Did you know anything about her?'

'Not a thing.' Sam chuckled. 'And more to the point, neither did any of the others. There hadn't been as much as a whisper about it.'

'Well, good luck to him. I just hope it works out this time.'

As they drove, the darkness of the night sky was punctuated by bursts of stars from the occasional rocket or the smouldering glow from the remains of back garden bonfires. The silence between them was easy and companionable.

'Denis certainly did a good job with the fireworks,' said Sam at last. 'The kids had a great time.' He paused as he reached a deserted road junction. 'It was nice to see Leonard there as well.'

Maggie threw Sam a sidelong glance and, unbeknown to him, in the darkness of the car was able to study his profile. Their relationship had subtly changed in the last weeks. Maggie was well aware of that, just as she knew that Sam was also aware of it. They had grown closer, and gradually she'd realised that she was falling in love with Sam. If she'd had any doubts before, they'd been finally dispelled during the evening, seeing Sam at Mill House together with his children and her own as he'd helped her entertain their friends.

As yet this new state of awareness between them had remained unspoken, but now as they sat alone together in Sam's car Maggie wondered if it was the perfect opportunity to tell him how she felt. There was a very good chance that Sam was still unsure of her and was holding back from making any further move after that moment on the beach when she'd all but rejected him, so Maggie had the feeling it was now down to her to set matters straight between them. She was on the verge of saying something when she realised that Sam had stopped the car.

'Here we are,' he said, leaning forward and looking up at the house.

'Oh, yes.' Maggie gave a little sigh. What she'd been about to say would have to wait. Bob Harrington had obviously been on the lookout for them for before they had a chance to even get out of the car he'd flung open his front door and hurried down the path.

Bending down, he looked into the car then stood back as Sam opened the door. 'Oh, Dr Neville—*and* Dr Hudson. Thank God. I thought they'd send some doctor who doesn't know Nadine.'

'What is it, Bob?' asked Maggie as she climbed out of the car. 'What's happened?'

'She's in a terrible state, Dr Hudson.' Bob was clearly highly agitated himself as he led the way into the house. 'It's been coming on for days. She's been very depressed again. She wouldn't even go to her counselling—in fact, she wouldn't go out at all. She'd got it into her head that someone was coming to get her. She was like this before, at the time she was watching the documentaries on the Kosovan war. She used to sit and cry for hours about those people driven from their homes—she seemed convinced that was going to happen to her.'

'Has she been taking her medication, Bob?' asked Maggie as he shut the front door behind Sam and herself.

'Oh, yes. I make sure of that, but the trouble now is that she's locked herself in the spare bedroom and she's got a whole month's supply of her tablets in there with her and a bottle of whisky that I'd put by for Christmas. You know she tried this once before, Dr Hudson, several years ago...' He trailed off helplessly.

'Have you any idea what triggered this tonight?' asked Sam.

'It was the fireworks,' explained Bob. 'I'd warned her there would be fireworks but when they started in next door's garden she just went to pieces. It was those firecrackers that did it. They were so loud. Poor Nadine thought it was gunfire and that it was gunmen come to get her. I did my best to reason with her but she was beyond it. All she was saying was that she didn't want to live if that was what was going to happen to her. I can't get her to come out of the bedroom and there hasn't been a sound from in there. I didn't know what else to do. I thought about ringing the police but I thought if they arrived it would only frighten her even more. She trusts you,

Dr Hudson—I thought you might be able to talk her round. But when I phoned they said you weren't on duty and it would be some other doctor...'

'It probably would have been,' said Maggie, 'if it wasn't Bonfire Night. As it is, the emergency on-call doctor is stretched to the limit and has asked us to help out.'

'Well, I've never been more pleased to see anyone in my life, I can tell you.' Bob ran a hand through his thinning hair.

'Right, let's go upstairs and see if we can talk to Nadine,' said Maggie.

Together the three of them climbed the stairs and Maggie and Sam waited on the landing whilst Bob knocked on a closed bedroom door. 'Nadine,' he called gently. 'Nadine, love, Dr Hudson is here, she wants to talk to you. Dr Neville is with her as well. Will you open the door?'

There was no sound from inside the bedroom. Bob turned to the two doctors and helplessly wrung his hands. 'You see?' he said.

'Let me try.' Maggie stepped forward. 'Nadine,' she called through the closed door. 'Nadine, it's me, Dr Hudson. I want to talk to you—but it's a bit difficult through this door. Won't you open it so that we can talk properly?'

Still there was only silence from within the bedroom.

'Nadine,' Maggie went on after a moment, 'Bob tells me you've been worried about things you've seen on television. Those things were dreadful, Nadine, but that war is over now, you know, and the things that you saw certainly aren't going to happen to you. I know you thought you heard gunfire this evening, but it wasn't guns—it was only fireworks. No one is after you, Nadine, you must believe me.'

The silence seemed more profound than ever and Bob looked at Maggie in despair.

'Let me try,' murmured Sam. 'Nadine—it's Dr Neville,' he called through the closed door. 'Remember you came to see me once when Dr Hudson was away? We want to help you, Nadine, but we can't do that unless you come out. Will you unlock the door for us? Please, Nadine.'

'She's so quiet,' muttered Bob. 'It's almost as if she isn't in there… Oh, lord, you don't think she's…?' He trailed off, unable to finish the sentence so great was his anguish.

'Nadine.' Maggie tried again. 'Is there anyone whom you would talk to? Would you like us to fetch your counsellor…or anyone else?'

When the silence persisted Sam looked at the other two. 'I think we need to get in,' he said quietly. 'We'll have to break the door down, Bob.'

'Yes, all right! Whatever.'

'I'll put my shoulder to the door,' said Sam, 'but first I'll tell Nadine what I'm going to do.'

'Is that wise?' asked Bob doubtfully.

'The shock of breaking through the door could do even more harm,' replied Sam. 'Don't you agree, Maggie?'

'Absolutely,' said Maggie. 'The alternative is that we call the police or the fire brigade but, to be honest, I don't feel inclined to leave it any longer.'

Bob took a deep breath then nodded. 'Right,' he said.

'Nadine,' called Maggie. 'Dr Neville is going to break the door open, but you mustn't be afraid.'

Sam stood back then with some considerable force put his shoulder to the door. It gave way at the second attempt.

The room beyond was in darkness and as Sam stood

aside Maggie groped her way into the room and fumbled for the light switch. Luckily the bulb was of low wattage and the light that suffused the room was dim. Maggie looked around her and at first glance it looked as if the room was empty. For a moment she thought that Bob had been mistaken and that his wife wasn't in the bedroom after all.

But as her eyes became accustomed to the dimness, she saw that the duvet had been pulled from one of the single beds and was stuffed down in the space between the beds. On lifting one edge of the duvet, Maggie realised that Nadine was curled up in a foetal position underneath.

'Nadine. Oh, Nadine,' she said quietly. 'It's all right. It's only me—Dr Hudson. Don't be afraid.'

But Nadine was beyond being afraid of anyone as the empty tablet bottle and the half-empty bottle of whisky on the bedside cabinet showed.

'She's taken the tablets,' said Maggie urgently over her shoulder to Sam. 'Phone for an ambulance.'

'Oh, no,' moaned Bob as he sank down onto the bed and covered his face with his hands. 'Oh, Nady… no, no, not again.'

While Sam phoned for the ambulance Maggie eased Nadine out from under the duvet. She was very drowsy and was muttering incoherently. Her hair was matted, there was saliva on her face and her breath smelt strongly of alcohol.

'Ambulance is on its way,' said Sam, coming over to assist Maggie.

'You think she needs sectioning, don't you?' Bob sounded almost accusing as Maggie and Sam set about trying to keep Nadine awake.

'Yes, Bob. I'm sorry, but I think she does,' Maggie replied. 'It won't be the first time so you know what to expect. The hospital will sort it out for you but you can be sure if she does have a spell in hospital, she'll get the help she needs.'

'Will she have to have her stomach pumped?'

'Yes, she will,' Maggie replied.

'I really didn't think she'd do this again,' said Bob. 'Not after the last time.'

The ambulance arrived very quickly and bore Nadine and Bob away to hospital, leaving Maggie and Sam to lock up the house and return to Sam's car.

'I should have spotted how bad she was,' said Maggie as Sam turned the car round.

'How could you have known?' he said.

'I'd asked her to come back for a follow-up appointment…she hasn't been. I suppose I should have checked up on her…'

'Maggie, we can't possibly be expected to chase up everyone who fails to make an appointment.'

'No, I suppose not.' Maggie sighed. 'Do you think she'll pull through?'

'Yes, I think so.' Sam nodded. 'Good thing we got there when we did. Another hour…' He shook his head, leaving the sentence unfinished. 'Did you know all that about the Kosovan war?' he added curiously after a few moments.

'No, neither of them had mentioned it to me,' Maggie replied. 'Nadine may have told her counsellor but if she had, I would have thought it would have been included in the counsellor's reports. I certainly don't remember seeing anything. Poor old Bob. I fear he's had a pretty rough ride just lately.'

'Well, hopefully something can be sorted out now,' Sam replied.

They drove on in silence and had almost reached Mill

House when Maggie remembered her earlier intention of telling Sam of her feelings. But whereas before, directly after the party, she had been fired up and ready to tell him, now, with the events of the past hour, her mood had changed and she found herself hesitating over what she should say.

She frowned in the darkness. She could hardly announce the fact right out of the blue that she'd decided after all that she felt something for him. If she did, she couldn't help wondering how he'd react. She threw him a surreptitious glance but his profile was set as he concentrated on negotiating the car down the narrow track.

Maybe he would react with horrified amazement or embarrassment or, and perish the thought, maybe he would laugh. After all, there was no way of knowing how he would have reacted if she'd responded to him that day on the beach. Perhaps that had simply been a one-off, a spur-of-the-moment impulse, and afterwards he may have regarded it as a single moment of folly.

On the other hand, maybe he would react with undisguised delight, would stop the car, switch off the engine and take her in his arms in a surge of wild, uncontrollable passion. At the thought of that, something stirred deep inside her—some half-forgotten urge, which until just lately Maggie had despaired of ever feeling again. Her heart began to beat faster and she ran her tongue around her lips, which had become uncomfortably dry. She looked at Sam's hands, one on the gear lever and the other on the wheel—strong, capable hands which she'd seen countless times before. Only now she found herself imagining them on her body, and they took on a new, exciting significance.

He brought the car to a halt and Maggie realised her pulse was racing.

It was now or never.

'Sam…' she began tentatively, but she got no further for Sam was looking at his watch in the light from the lamp on the side of the house and gave a muttered exclamation.

'Is that the time? I promised Fiona I'd run her home. I wonder if the kids have gone to bed. It was good of you to let them sleep over…' He paused as Maggie climbed out of the car. 'Maggie, were you about to say something?'

'Sorry?' said Maggie.

'Just now, I thought you were about to say something. I'm afraid I interrupted you.'

'No,' Maggie replied quickly. 'No, you didn't. It's all right, Sam, it wasn't anything.' Suddenly, for some reason, the moment had gone and Maggie no longer felt able to say what she'd been planning.

Together they went into the house, where they found Ingrid clearing up after the party and Fiona sitting on the sofa, flipping through the pages of a glossy magazine.

'The children are in bed,' called Ingrid. 'I doubt whether they're asleep—that would be too much to hope for.'

'I'll go up and say goodnight to them,' said Sam. 'And then, Fiona…' he looked down at the woman on the sofa '…I must get you home.'

Maggie joined Ingrid in the kitchen. 'You've done nearly all of it,' she said, looking around. 'You really are a treasure, Ingrid.'

'It doesn't take long once you get stuck in,' said Ingrid.

A few moments later Sam came downstairs and Fiona tossed the magazine aside and jumped to her feet.

'I'll ring you tomorrow, Maggie, about picking up the

children,' said Sam. Suddenly he looked impossibly handsome, standing there in his sweater and jeans.

'Yes, all right, Sam,' she heard herself say. What she really wanted to say was, Stay. Stay here, Sam, with me and our children where you belong. But, of course, she said nothing of the sort because in the past Sam had never stayed the night at Mill House even when his children had slept over. Instead, she said, 'Thanks for all your help tonight.'

'Don't mention it. It was a pleasure.' He smiled. 'Goodnight, Maggie. Goodnight, Ingrid.'

Maggie walked to the door with Sam and Fiona. After bidding them both goodnight, she watched as Fiona climbed into the passenger seat of Sam's car while he took his place behind the wheel. With a wave of his hand they were gone and Maggie turned and walked back into the house, swamped by a sudden feeling of anticlimax. She had wanted to tell Sam about her feelings, had really worked herself up to do so, but she knew now that it was going to have to wait until another time.

Ingrid was packing china into the kitchen cupboards. 'Are you all right, Maggie?' she asked, throwing her a keen glance as she came in.

'Yes, I guess I'm tired, that's all,' said Maggie with a sigh. 'But it was a good party, wasn't it, Ingrid?'

'Oh, yes.'

'I think everyone enjoyed themselves.' Maggie began sorting out the cutlery.

'Some more than others,' retorted Ingrid.

Maggie looked up quickly and saw a tight-lipped expression on Ingrid's face. 'Well, it was nice to meet the new lady in Dr Turner's life,' she said when Ingrid remained silent.

Ingrid nodded. 'Yes,' she agreed. 'She seemed nice.'

'I have to say I was surprised,' said Maggie. 'I thought Jon and Fiona might have had a thing going…'

'Oh, no.' Ingrid pulled a face. 'That one has her sights set higher than the junior partner.'

Maggie stopped what she was doing and stared at Ingrid. 'What do you mean?' she said.

'Well, her and Dr Neville…' Ingrid replied.

'What about her and Dr Neville?' asked Maggie.

'It's pretty obvious, isn't it?' said Ingrid.

'What is?' Suddenly everything in the kitchen seemed very still, every colour heightened as if time had been suspended.

'She's after him,' said Ingrid. 'I would go so far as to say it's been that way ever since she set foot in Millbury, and if what she said tonight was anything to go by, I'd say she was succeeding.'

Maggie stared at Ingrid and as the meaning of what she was saying sank in a sudden wave of nausea washed over her. In an attempt to ignore it she said, 'What exactly did she say?' She was amazed at how calm she sounded.

'It was after the two of you went off on the house call,' Ingrid replied. 'She said she was going to wait for him. I told her you could be gone some time and I offered to call a taxi, but she said, no, that if she went home by taxi she would be disappointing Dr Neville.'

'Disappointing Dr Neville?' echoed Maggie weakly.

'Yes, and there was no mistaking what she meant,' said Ingrid darkly. 'She even went on to say what a coincidence it was that both Dr Neville and Dr Turner were involved in new relationships at the same time. I have to say I'm disappointed…' She threw Maggie a quick, searching glance but Maggie was so stunned she was unable to reply. 'I was living in the hope that it would be you and Dr Neville getting together one day.'

'Oh, Dr Neville and I are just good friends,' Maggie said wildly at last, finding her voice from somewhere.

'I know you're good friends.' Ingrid sniffed. 'And I suppose that's why you seemed so right together. And then there're the children…you all seem to get on so well. Even my mother said tonight that you seemed just like one big happy family. Oh, well, never mind.' She shrugged. 'I suppose you can't arrange these things to order. But I have to say I can't somehow imagine Dr Neville with that Fiona Winn…'

What a fool she'd been. What she'd believed to be a growing relationship between Sam and herself had been nothing of the sort. Even the pass she thought he'd made at her that day on the beach had, no doubt, been little more than a figment of her imagination. Thank God she hadn't said anything, she thought miserably. Imagine the embarrassment, the utter humiliation, if she'd told Sam that she thought she might be falling in love with him, only for him to have to put her down—albeit ever so gently, for the infliction of pain didn't feature heavily in Sam's agenda whatever the situation—when he explained that he and Fiona were an item.

Maggie felt as if the bottom had dropped out of her world when Ingrid had told her, and afterwards she was to curse herself for not having seen it before. She'd known there was a new man in Fiona's life—Fiona herself had told her but she'd assumed it was Jon. Even when Jon had introduced Beverley to her and she'd realised that Jon and Fiona weren't the item she'd believed them to be, it still hadn't occurred to her who Fiona's man was.

Later, when she'd somehow managed to finish clearing up after the party, had said goodnight to Ingrid and gained the sanctuary of her room, there was still no respite from her anguish for the realisation had then dawned that it had all been happening right under her nose. It had probably been happening that Sunday when she'd found Fiona at Sam's house when she'd assumed that they'd been discussing practice business. And it had certainly been happening when Fiona had asked her to prescribe the Pill for her. It had been going on on those occasions when she'd been unable to contact Sam and it had certainly been going on here tonight under her very own roof—that closeness she'd seen between them in the garage and again later while they'd been watching the fireworks. Oh, how could she have been so blind?

And Fiona had been waiting for him when they'd returned from their house call. No chance that she might have accepted a lift home from anyone else—and there would have been plenty travelling in her direction. No, she'd been there sitting on Maggie's sofa, looking cool and glamorous as she'd waited for Sam to come and take her home.

But maybe she only had herself to blame, Maggie agonised, for hadn't she rejected Sam and hadn't she herself told Fiona there was nothing between herself and Sam and that they were no more than good friends?

She spent a miserable night, lying awake for hours tossing and turning as images of Sam and Fiona together filled her mind. He would have gone to her flat and, of course, she would have invited him inside. She would probably have made coffee or maybe in their haste they would have dispensed with the niceties and hurtled headlong into a passionate encounter. They would inevitably have ended up in Fiona's bedroom or maybe they'd made love in front of the fire. At the thought of that her heart twisted in torment and kept her from sleeping. When at last, exhausted, she did fall into a troubled sleep the image of them together haunted her dreams.

'Mum, you look awful.'

'Thanks, Jessica. You certainly know how to cheer me up.'

'Are you ill?' Jessica peered across the breakfast table. It was the following morning and the four children, William and Jessica and Richard and Emma, were seated around the breakfast table whilst Ingrid cooked scrambled eggs.

'No, I'm not ill,' Maggie replied, aware that she'd become the main object of scrutiny. 'I just didn't sleep very well, that's all.'

'It was a good party,' said Richard solemnly.

'Thank you, Richard,' Maggie replied. 'Yes, it was a good party.'

'Can we take the dogs out?' asked Emma.

'Well, I'm not sure what time your father is coming for you.' Maggie turned to the Aga and poured herself a large mug of hot, black coffee. He'll probably be late, she thought miserably. No doubt, Fiona would want a lie-in…

'Could we take the dogs just until he does come?' Emma persisted.

'And what if we're miles away across the fields somewhere?' said Richard. 'We won't know when he comes, will we? He promised he'd take me to choose a microscope today for my birthday.'

'Why don't you phone him?' said William.

Maggie didn't answer. There was no way she was going to phone Sam that morning. Richard could do so if he wanted but she wasn't going to.

In the end no one had to do anything for the phone rang and Jessica went to answer it.

'It's Sam,' she said. 'He wants to speak to you, Mum.'

Maggie took the phone from her daughter and walked to the window. 'Sam?' she said.

'Oh, Maggie.' He sounded faintly surprised, as if he'd caught the coolness in her tone. 'Good morning. Have you recovered?'

'Of course,' she replied frostily. 'Have you?'

'Yes, just about.' He paused. 'Look, Maggie, I'm at the centre.'

'Really?' So he wasn't still in bed with Fiona. 'But isn't Jon on duty this morning?' The three of them took turns to do Saturday morning surgeries and she couldn't imagine why Sam was there.

'Yes, he is. I called in early to collect some notes, but I'm rather concerned about Aimee.'

'Aimee? Why, what's wrong with her?'

'I'm not sure. She was on duty with Jon this morning but she's, well… look Maggie, I don't really want to discuss this over the phone. I was wondering…could you come in, do you think?'

'I should think so. What about the children?'

'Is Ingrid there?'

'Yes.'

'Do you think she would mind if they stayed with her for an hour?'

'I shouldn't think so. I'll ask her.'

Turning from the window, she looked at Ingrid.

'Is there a problem?' asked Ingrid.

'Sam wants me to go into the centre, Ingrid. It'll only be for about an hour.'

'No problem.' Ingrid began serving large portions of scrambled eggs onto rounds of hot buttered toast. 'We'll take the dogs for a walk.'

'What about my microscope?' said Richard anxiously.

'Richard says, what about his microscope?' said Maggie into the mouthpiece.

'Oh, lord, I'd forgotten about that,' Sam replied. 'Tell him I'll sort it out later this morning.'

'Your dad says he'll sort it out later this morning,' said Maggie as she replaced the receiver. That seemed to satisfy Richard as the prospect of a ramble with the dogs seemed to satisfy the others.

Maggie grabbed a piece of toast spread it sparingly with butter and liberally with marmalade and took it and her mug of coffee upstairs to her bedroom where she pulled on a thick sweater over her shirt and cords, brushed out the unruly mass of her hair and applied just a light touch of make-up.

So he wasn't with Fiona this morning, she told herself as she prepared to leave for the centre. She'd been wrong about that, but it didn't mean to say that he hadn't stayed the night at Fiona's flat and left at the crack of dawn. She couldn't imagine why he wanted her to go in to the centre. Something to do with Aimee he'd said, but Aimee had been fine only the evening before and had appeared to be enjoying the party along with Denis and the children. It was an unusual request for Sam to make and Maggie found both her curiosity and her apprehension growing as she drove into Millbury, curiosity over Aimee and apprehension over seeing Sam after his supposed night of passion.

As she drove into the car park of the medical centre it briefly crossed her mind that Fiona also might have decided to come into work that morning. Fervently Maggie hoped that wasn't the case. Quite suddenly she found herself unable to cope with seeing the two of them together.

Which, when she really considered it, was ridiculous, for if Sam and Fiona were indeed an item then she would have to get used to seeing them together in every conceivable situation, both professionally and socially. The very thought caused her to shudder but in a desperate attempt to pull herself together, and at the same time trying to ignore the situation which seemed to be unfolding before her, Maggie got out of the car and locked it.

Sam's car was parked alongside Jon's, and on the far side of the car park Maggie was surprised to see Dawn's car parked alongside Aimee's. They only ever had one practice nurse on duty on a Saturday morning, and as far as Maggie was aware it was Aimee's turn on this particular Saturday.

She entered the building to find Jackie on duty in Reception, a strangely subdued Jackie.

'Oh, Dr Hudson.' Jackie looked up from the appointment book. 'You're here as well.' Lowering her voice so that the patients in the waiting room couldn't hear, she said, 'What in the world is going on this morning? We now have no less than three doctors and two nurses here, and on a Saturday—that's more than we have sometimes on a busy Monday morning.'

'I don't know, Jackie.' Maggie shook her head. 'But that's what I'm here to find out. Where's Dr Neville?'

'He was in the staffroom with Aimee but he said I had to let him know when you arrived.' As she spoke she pressed a switch. 'Oh, Dr Neville,' she said, 'Dr Hudson has just arrived. Yes. Very well, I'll do that.' She looked at Maggie. 'He said could you join him in his room.'

'Of course.' Squaring her shoulders but more mystified than ever, Maggie made her way to Sam's consulting room.

CHAPTER ELEVEN

SAM looked up from his desk as Maggie came into his
consulting room. She looked tired, which was understandable after the party the night before, and his heart went
out to her. He knew she'd put a lot of effort into the
preparations and he wished desperately that he hadn't had
to bother her this morning. But sometimes there were
things that simply couldn't be shelved, and unfortunately
this was one of those times.

'Sam…?' Maggie frowned, but in spite of her anxious
expression and her apparent tiredness she still looked attractive in that gipsy-like way which was both bohemian
and romantic and so essentially Maggie.

'I'm sorry about this, Maggie. You know I wouldn't
have called you in unless I thought it was strictly necessary.'

'Has something happened to Aimee?' Maggie looked
around the room as if she expected to find the practice
nurse sitting in a corner.

'You could say that.' Sam nodded. 'When I called in
this morning Jon came in here and told me that there was
something wrong with Aimee. He said when she arrived
at the centre this morning he thought at first she'd been
mugged—'

'Sam—no!' Maggie looked aghast.

'He said he'd questioned her but she wouldn't tell him
what had happened. I then went into the treatment room
myself and found Aimee,' Sam went on. 'She has a badly
bruised face and I suspect she has other injuries to her

body. She didn't want to talk at first so I immediately took her off duty and phoned Dawn to take her place. I told her I was calling you as well, and I'm hoping she'll be able to talk to you.'

'Have you any idea what's happened?' asked Maggie slowly.

'I know what I think might have happened,' replied Sam, 'but, of course, we can't know for sure. I would say she's suffered a serious assault.'

'Have you any theories?'

'Yes, I do. In fact, it occurred to me last night at the party what might be happening.'

'You think it's Denis, don't you?' Maggie stared at him, and when he nodded she said, 'I thought they all seemed OK last night—as a family, I mean.'

'I thought there was a lot of hidden tension,' said Sam. 'I watched the children. Melanie didn't really want to mix with the other children and I thought Josh seemed very wary when his father was around.'

'And Aimee?' said Maggie slowly.

'She was *too* happy—bright and brittle, like she was about to shatter.'

'If this is the case, I can hardly believe it.' Maggie shook her head. 'I know there was that report from the school about Josh, and Jessica told me that Melanie is odd, but I really didn't think there was anything to worry about. Oh, heavens, Sam, do you think this was a one-off?'

Sam stood up and turned to the window. 'I doubt it. Think about it, Maggie. Aimee has been off sick quite a bit and there was her broken arm—'

'You don't think...' Maggie looked up sharply. 'Oh, Sam, this is appalling. We must do something. We must get to the bottom of it—we must try and help Aimee.'

'I know. Believe me, I feel the same as you. But we have to tread carefully. You know as well as I do what these cases are like—we've seen it all before. If it is Denis, and we don't know for sure that it is, Aimee may well not want to admit it. And even if she does, she may not feel able to bring charges against him, in which case, as you well know, it will almost certainly happen again.'

'I'd better go and talk to her,' said Maggie slowly.

'She's in the staffroom.' Sam turned from the window. 'I'll come with you.'

Together they left Sam's consulting room and made their way to the staffroom. Maggie could hardly believe what Sam had just told her...and yet if it was indeed true then it added up.

For a while the seriousness of the situation outweighed the anguish she'd been feeling over Sam and Fiona, and she was forced to put that on hold as they faced this very human drama within their own staff.

Aimee was sitting in a low armchair by the window in the staffroom. She didn't as much as look up as the two doctors came into the room but Maggie noticed that her thin hands were curled around a mug of coffee.

'Aimee.' Maggie moved round in front of her and crouched down, and it was then that she saw the huge bruise on the side of her face which encircled her eye and stretched down below her cheek almost to her jaw. 'Oh, Aimee,' she said softly.

Aimee did look up then, and as her gaze met Maggie's a single tear trickled down her bruised cheek.

'Aimee, do you want to tell me about this?' asked Maggie gently. She glanced up at Sam.

'Would you like me to go?' he said quietly. 'Perhaps, Aimee, you'd like to talk to Maggie on your own.'

'No, it's all right.' Aimee shook her head then winced

as if the movement hurt her. 'I'm sure you've drawn your own conclusions anyway.'

'They may not be the right conclusions,' said Maggie. 'But first, Aimee, why don't I have a look at your bruises?' Leaning forward, she carefully examined the bruised and swollen area on Aimee's face.

'Do you want to see the others?' asked Aimee when Maggie had finished. Her voice was dull now, almost devoid of emotion.

'I think I'd better,' Maggie replied. She was about to suggest that Aimee come down to her examination room, but before she had the chance to do so Aimee had unbuttoned her uniform, slipping it off her shoulder to reveal yet more bruising, this time covering an area from her shoulder to below her ribs.

'Does it feel as if any bones are broken?' asked Maggie.

'No.' Aimee shook her head. 'Not this time.'

'The thing is, Aimee, do you intend doing anything about it?' asked Sam gently.

'If you'd asked me that before, I would have said no,' Aimee replied.

'And now?' asked Maggie as she pulled up Aimee's uniform and buttoned it for her.

'It's different now. I've had time to think and you see…everything's changed.' Aimee took a deep breath. 'I took the children to my parents early this morning,' she went on after a moment, 'like I do every Saturday when I'm on duty, but when we got there…' She swallowed and seemed unable to go on.

'What happened when you got there?' urged Maggie gently.

'My…my mother asked what had happened to my face,' said Aimee.

'And?'

'I was all set to lie as I usually do—you know, I'd tripped or walked into a door, that sort of thing…but…'

'What happened this time, Aimee?'

'It was Josh. He…he told them what had happened. He just came right out with it. He said, "Daddy did it—he hit Mummy. He's always hitting Mummy. I want you to make him stop."'

'So what happened then?' asked Sam.

'Melanie burst into tears, my mother nearly had hysterics and my father…well, he went mad. He's an ex-policeman and there's no way he's going to take this lying down. He demanded to know the truth.'

'So did you tell him?' said Maggie.

'Yes, I told them what happened last night after the party and about some of the other times,' Aimee said at last. She was silent for a while as if reflecting on all those other dreadful times. 'I didn't think the children knew…' she went on at last. 'I tried never to make a sound so they wouldn't know…but…but they knew…' Fresh tears filled her eyes and ran unheeded down her cheeks.

'How long, Aimee? How long has it been happening?' asked Maggie.

'For as long as I can remember.' Aimee's voice was barely more than a whisper and both Maggie and Sam had to strain to hear what she was saying. 'It…it started on our honeymoon…that was the first time. We've been married for nearly thirteen years and I've lost count of the number of times since…'

A shocked silence followed Aimee's admission then Maggie spoke again. 'What triggers it?' she asked. 'Is there anything in particular?'

'He's so jealous,' Aimee replied. 'If another man as much as looks at me he goes mad.'

'So what was last night about?' Maggie frowned.

'Would you believe because of Dr Ward?'

'Leonard?' said Maggie in amazement. 'Whatever has he got to do with it?'

'Ridiculous, isn't it?' Aimee's voice had grown stronger, bitter now in its tone. 'But that's how it is. Dr Ward and I stood together, watching the fireworks, then as we went back into the house he put his arm around me. It was just a fatherly gesture—after all, I've known him and worked with him for years—but I knew Denis would go mad if he'd seen it and I hoped and prayed that he was so busy with the fireworks that he hadn't.'

'But obviously he had. Is that what you're saying?' asked Sam incredulously.

'Oh, yes,' said Aimee bitterly. 'He'd seen all right. And to make matters worse, he started drinking—he's always ten times worse when he's been drinking...' She trailed off and Maggie and Sam looked at each other.

'Your broken arm,' said Sam after a moment. 'Did he do that?'

Aimee nodded. 'Yes, that was because he caught me talking to one of his colleagues. The poor man was only helping me to pack my groceries but Denis made up his mind we were having an affair... I told everyone I'd fallen off my bicycle... Another time was after you came to the house that Sunday, Maggie—he went mad because I hadn't told him about the party. He thought I was planning to go without him. On that occasion I felt so ill afterwards I had to pretend I had a migraine and couldn't come in to work.'

'Did you never think of saying anything before?' asked Maggie.

'Oh, yes, I thought about it,' Aimee replied bitterly, 'lots of times. But actually doing it is another matter. I couldn't see beyond it. What would happen...to us...as a family, I mean. I loved Denis, you see. He's my husband—he's the father of my children. He loves them and they love him, and I know it sounds crazy…but I believe in his own way he…he loves me. After these episodes he is always so sorry…' Her voice faltered.

'Until the next time,' said Maggie quietly.

'Yes, until the next time,' Aimee agreed. 'And I know there will always be a next time. Even if we could stop him drinking…which I doubt…I don't think his jealousy could be cured.' She paused then took a deep breath. 'I…I reached a decision just now while I was sitting here… I think it was seeing Josh so upset that did it…and Melanie…she was distressed as well. It was bad enough when it was just me…but I thought I could hide it then and no one would know, but now that the children are affected…'

'What have you decided?' asked Sam. He had perched on the edge of the large coffee-table, his hands clasped loosely between his knees as he gravely contemplated Aimee.

'I want a separation,' she replied.

'I think that's probably the only decision in these circumstances,' Sam agreed quietly.

'It won't be easy,' said Maggie.

'I know that,' Aimee nodded. 'He won't want to go and I dare say I'll have to take out an injunction against him, but I've made up my mind. We can't go on like this.'

'What about the immediate future?' asked Maggie.

'I'm going to leave the children at my parents' and I'll stay there, too, until Denis leaves the house. If he tries to bother me, I shall call the police and bring charges against him for assault. I know I'll have my parents' support in this.'

'And you know you can rely on us for any other help or support you may need,' said Sam.

'Thank you,' whispered Aimee. 'Thank you…'

'I think you should take some time off work—don't you agree, Maggie?' Sam threw her a quick glance.

'Absolutely,' Maggie replied firmly. 'At least a couple of weeks to get everything sorted out—longer if you need it.'

'But how will you manage? Dawn can't do any more hours.' Aimee looked worried.

'Don't worry about that. If necessary we'll get a bank nurse in to cover for you. You just concentrate on yourself and your children and what you have to do.'

'I think you should return to your parents' home now,' said Sam gently. 'Would you like me to drive you there?'

'Oh, no.' Aimee shook her head. 'I have my car. I'm all right—really I am. In fact, if I'm honest I think I'm starting to feel better than I have for a very long time.'

'That's because you've reached a decision,' said Maggie.

As the door closed behind Aimee, Sam and Maggie looked at each other.

'I can still hardly believe it,' said Maggie at last. 'Who would have thought it?'

'It certainly explains everything, and now that we know that the children were aware of what was going on it could account for Josh's behaviour problems and Melanie's apparent oddness and reluctance to join in with the other children.'

'Do you think he'll leave her alone?' asked Maggie doubtfully.

'Denis?' Sam shrugged. 'Goodness knows—but let's hope so. It may have shamed him now that it's out in the open. I can't imagine he will be too happy for his mates in the fire service to know what a bully he is—or his colleagues at the supermarket, come to that.'

'Do you think we should have suggested a place of safety order for the children or even a refuge for Aimee herself?'

'It did cross my mind.' Sam answered, 'but it sounds to me as if they'll be all right at her parents'—and with her dad being an ex-copper, he'll know the procedures if it comes to court orders or injunctions.'

'It's so sad when it comes to this for a family,' said Maggie, shaking her head.

'I agree,' Sam replied. 'But it couldn't go on—and somehow I doubt whether he'd change. No one has the right to treat anyone like that, least of all his own wife. No, I fear our Denis only has himself to blame.'

'I feel sorry for the children.'

'Maybe. But they're better off away from that. Seeing their mother hurt and humiliated like that must have been having a devastating effect on them.' As he finished speaking Sam stood up. 'Thanks for coming in, Maggie. I really do appreciate it.'

'Not at all. It's the least I could do and I'm glad you called me. But I suppose I'd better get back to the children now. Ingrid will be wondering where I've got to.' She paused. 'What are you going to do, Sam?'

'I have to take Richard to get his microscope.'

'Oh, yes, of course. What about afterwards? Are you coming back for lunch?'

'I would have loved to, Maggie, but I have to get the children back to Claire. Thanks all the same.'

'That's OK,' she replied lightly. 'It was just a thought.' Probably what he really meant was that he had to get the children home so that he could meet Fiona again. Her heart twisted painfully at the thought. Just for a while there, while they'd been immersed in Aimee's problems, she'd forgotten Fiona and the fact that Sam and she had, no doubt, spent the previous night together, but now the thoughts were back to torment her afresh. Miserably she turned to go but Sam called her back.

'Oh, Maggie,' he said, 'just one other thing—a bit of good news, actually.'

'Well, that'll make a change—what is it?'

'There was a call from the hospital soon after I got here this morning—Jon put it through to me. Nadine is OK.'

'That's a relief.'

'She had her stomach pumped, of course, and apparently she's been transferred to a psychiatric ward for further assessment.'

'Good,' Maggie replied. 'Let's hope this time she gets the help she needs.'

Together they left the medical centre, after explaining about Aimee to Jon and Dawn and leaving them to cope with the rest of the morning's problems, before driving separately to Mill House.

After a quick coffee Sam left with Richard and Emma, and as she watched them drive away Maggie felt a moment of total desolation. He was going out of her life, she knew it, and there seemed little or nothing she could do to stop it. He'd fallen for Fiona and she for him and all she could do was to stand back and watch their romance unfold before her eyes.

'What's the matter, Mum?' Jessica was at her elbow and to her horror Maggie realised there were tears in her eyes and that her daughter had seen them.

'Nothing, darling,' she said, dashing the tears away with her hand.

'There must be something,' Jessica persisted. 'You don't cry for nothing. Is it Dad?'

Maggie considered. It would have been easy to have said yes and have left it at that. Jessica would have accepted that. 'Actually, no,' she said at last. 'This time I don't think it was. It usually is, but not this time.'

'Why did you have to go to work?' asked Jessica. 'Are you allowed to say?' she added hurriedly. She knew only too well about confidentiality.

'Not all of it,' Maggie admitted. Slipping an arm around her daughter's shoulders as Sam's car disappeared into the lane at the top of the track, they turned to go back into the house. 'It was to do with the Barnes family,' she said. 'They're having a lot of problems at the moment.'

'So you'll be wanting me to be extra nice to Melanie,' said Jessica.

'Yes, I will.'

'Actually, she's not as bad as I thought,' said Jessica slowly. 'I really got talking to her last night and when you get to know her she's quite nice.'

'That's good—I think she'll be very glad of your friendship, especially at this time.'

'It's awful when something happens to your family,' said Jessica. 'Something different, I mean. It was like when Daddy died. I was the only one whose father had died and it was awful—nobody really understood.'

'I know, darling, I know.' Maggie gave her a hug. 'But sometimes, you know, I think we have to go through those bad times so that later on we can help someone else who's going through a bad time.'

'Like Melanie?'

'Yes, just like Melanie.'

'And Josh. Wills will have to help Josh. I'll go and tell him.'

As her daughter hurried away to find her brother Maggie once again felt the tears fill her eyes.

The following week at the medical centre proved to be fraught and full of problems. There was much speculation over Aimee and the reason why she was taking extended leave, and in the end Sam was forced to call an emergency staff meeting and with Aimee's consent offer a limited explanation. He told the assembled staff that Aimee and Denis were parting and that for the time being Aimee and the children were staying with her parents.

'I always thought there was something wrong there,' said Jackie as the staff filed out from the meeting. 'I never did like Denis—he was so fanatical. Aimee had to keep that house immaculate otherwise he'd go mad.'

'What do you suppose has happened?' asked Holly. 'Another woman?'

'Probably,' Jackie replied with a sniff. 'On the other hand, that wouldn't explain why Aimee's at her parents' with the children. No, I reckon there's more to it than that.'

'Shall we have a little less gossip and a bit more work?' Fiona broke into the girls' chatter and hurried them out of the staffroom, leaving the three doctors alone.

'I think I've just made things worse,' said Sam, running a hand over his hair.

'They had to be told something,' said Jon. 'And it wasn't exactly for us to say that Denis had been using Aimee as a punchbag. They'll find that out soon enough. News travels fast on this Island, as we well know…' He trailed off as the phone rang on the table behind him. He leaned back to pick it up. 'Katie. Yes?' He frowned, obviously listening as Katie spoke. 'All right, Katie,' he said at last. Pulling a face, he replaced the receiver and looked at the other two.

'What is it?' asked Maggie.

'Katie said Fiona and Jackie are in the middle of a furious argument in Reception.'

Sam groaned and Maggie put her head in her hands. 'Oh, no,' she sighed, 'not again. I suppose I'd better go and try and sort it out. I wonder what it's about this time.'

'No,' said Sam with a sigh, 'I'll go.'

Miserably Maggie watched him leave the staffroom. If there was any sort of problem involving Fiona then it stood to reason that Sam would be the one who would want to sort it out. After all, he wouldn't want her being upset in any way. As the door closed behind Sam she found herself thinking how much simpler life would have been in more ways than one if Fiona Winn had never applied for the job of practice manager at the Millbury Street Practice.

'Are you OK, Maggie?' asked Jon, suddenly breaking into her thoughts.

'Yes,' she lied. 'I'm fine.'

'It's just that this past week you don't seem to have been yourself.'

'Oh, I'm just a bit tired, that's all. First there was the party then there's been all the trouble with Aimee…and now all this wrangling with the staff…' She trailed off and Jon seemed to accept her explanation, but what she didn't say was that the real reason for her misery during the last week was the yawning gulf that had developed between herself and Sam and which, as time went on, she could only see growing wider as his relationship with Fiona deepened. The closeness they'd shared of late had all been in her head, with even those meaningful glances of no significance, and it almost broke Maggie's heart when she thought of how briefly she'd been so happy, only for it to be snatched away from her.

Later, through Katie, Maggie heard that Sam had managed to diffuse the most recent argument in Reception, although it sounded as if there was no guarantee it wouldn't flare up again at the slightest provocation from either side. This latest dispute had been over the allocation of extra appointments, which had resulted in an argument with an irate patient. Holly had got the blame from Fiona and had ended up in floods of tears. Katie had apparently pointed out that Holly had only been following Fiona's instructions and Jackie had leapt in, defending Holly and pointing out how flawed Fiona's system was anyway.

In the end Maggie was glad when it was time to go home. If she was honest, she was beginning to feel exhausted with her workload. In her heart she knew that full-time work was really too much for her even with Ingrid's help—she'd been much happier working part time and spending more time with the children. But that had been when David had been alive and in those days life had been very different. To make matters even worse, and adding to her exhaustion, there was her personal anguish over Sam and Fiona. So it was with a decided sense of relief that she reached Mill House, entered the welcoming warmth of her kitchen and shut the door on the world.

CHAPTER TWELVE

IT ALWAYS amazed Maggie how quickly the winter after-
noons drew in. It seemed that after lunch in no time at all
it was dusk and time to light the lamps and draw the
blinds. Because it was a Saturday Ingrid had gone to her
mother's and for once Maggie was alone at Mill House
as the children were attending a party and a disco at a
neighbour's house. She had taken the opportunity to catch
up on the mountain of paperwork she had recently taken
to carrying around with her from surgery to home and
back again in the vain hope that she might find a moment
to reduce it. She had, however, reached the stage where
she'd had enough. Replacing the cap on her pen, she
yawned and stretched.

A log fire had been blazing in the grate but it had died
down and, rising to her feet, Maggie crossed the room,
took a log from the stack alongside the fireplace and threw
it onto the fire. Leaning against the mantelpiece, she gazed
down into the grate and watched as tiny darts of blue and
orange flame licked around the pine log. She'd heard
nothing from Sam that day, but why would she? He'd
been on duty that morning, but no doubt, the rest of his
weekend was being spent with Fiona.

Oh, why hadn't she realised sooner how she felt about
Sam? Why couldn't she have let him know before he
became involved with Fiona?

With a sigh she straightened up and, moving to the
window, was about to draw the curtains when she caught
sight of the headlights of a car approaching Mill House

down the narrow track from the lane. She frowned, narrowing her eyes, wondering who it could be at this time of day. It was too early for either Ingrid or the children and she certainly wasn't expecting anyone else. It was too dark to see either the make or the colour of the car, but as it disappeared from her view, coming to a halt at the side of the house, Maggie was surprised that there was no sound from either of the dogs, which indicated that the driver was someone they knew.

A moment later there came a tap at the back door, again indicating that the caller was well known to the household—anyone else would have used the main front entrance of the house. And still there was no sound from the dogs as Maggie hurried to the door.

'It's all right, Maggie, it's only me.' No further identification was necessary—the voice was instantly recognisable. She pulled open the door and there he was, his face dear and smiling, the dogs on either side of him frantically wagging their tails.

'Sam. This is a surprise.' She tried not to let her joy at seeing him be too obvious. 'I wasn't expecting to see you today. Come in.' She stood aside and he brushed past her. It was as much as she could do to stop herself from throwing her arms around him, hugging him, but she couldn't do that. There was someone else in Sam's life now and it wouldn't do to forget it. Everything was about to change—the old easy familiarity there had been between them was about to disappear, probably to be replaced by a more formal, even stilted relationship, the thought of which filled her with anguish.

No doubt, this was why he'd come, to tell her about these changes, to tell her about the new life he was about to embark upon. As she shut the door behind him she shivered, but the sudden chill she felt had little to do with the damp darkness that surrounded Mill House.

'I'm sorry to disturb your peace.' Sam followed her into the sitting room and glanced at the fire and the table strewn with her paperwork, an empty coffee-mug in its midst.

'That's all right. I'd finished anyway—well, not finished exactly,' she corrected herself. 'I doubt whether I'd ever catch up on everything even if I worked all night—but I've certainly done enough for today.' She was starting to waffle, she knew, she could hear it in her voice, but suddenly she wanted to delay the moment when he told her why he'd come to see her.

'Maggie, I need to talk to you.' Sam had crossed to the fireplace but he turned now to face her.

'I was about to make some tea,' she said wildly. 'Would you like some?'

'I would love some tea, but later, Maggie. Let me talk to you first. There's something I need to tell you.'

'I know,' she said miserably. 'I know what you have to tell me.'

'Do you?' He looked faintly surprised.

'Yes, Sam…and…and all I can say is that I hope everything works out for you and that you'll be happy.'

'But—'

'You have to get on with your life. I told you that once before—you have to move on.'

'Well, yes, but—'

'And then there's the children. Maybe it will be better for them in the long run. Have you told them yet?'

'No…' He sounded slightly mystified now, but Maggie hardly paused for breath.

'But at least they've met her. I know they won't have

had time to get to know her properly yet, but all in good time…'

'Maggie, who are you talking about?' Gently he took her wrists and held her there, captive.

'Fiona, of course.' She looked at him. 'Who did you think I was talking about?'

'I really didn't know.' He paused. 'But why should you be talking about Fiona?'

'Wasn't that what you'd come to talk to me about? You and Fiona?'

'Me and Fiona…?' He stared at her for a long moment then, shaking his head slightly, he said, 'Why should you think that, Maggie?'

She gulped. 'I thought that you and she…you and she were…were an item.'

He stared at her then with a sound that resembled a groan he released her wrists before enfolding her in a fierce, protective hug. 'Oh, Maggie, Maggie,' he murmured.

'Sam,' she said at last, her voice muffled from the depths of his sweater, 'are you trying to tell me that you aren't?'

'Before I answer that, can I ask if it would bother you if we were?'

'Actually. Yes. It would.' She swallowed. 'I know I have no right to feel that way. But I can't bear to think that things will change.'

'And you think they might?'

'Well, they'd be bound to, wouldn't they? You couldn't keep coming here the way you have been. We wouldn't be able to go out together even with the children. It simply wouldn't work…would it? Not if there was someone else on the scene.'

'No,' he agreed. 'I doubt if it would. But what if there wasn't—someone else on the scene, I mean?'

'What do you mean?' Maggie looked bewildered.

'Well, would things change then?'

'Sam, I'm getting totally confused. Can we start again, please?'

'I think perhaps we'd better.'

'Did you come here to tell me that you and Fiona are an item?'

'No,' he said. 'Because we aren't.'

Her breath caught in her throat. 'But I thought you were.'

'I can't imagine why you should have thought that.' He shook his head.

'Well, Fiona... She seemed... She said... Oh, it doesn't matter what she said but, whatever it was, it left me feeling that you and she were about to embark on a grand passion.'

'I can assure you we aren't.'

'But does she know that?' Maggie was vaguely aware of a slow feeling of relief beginning to creep over her, just like the evening mist that stole through the valley and settled around the house.

'She does now.'

'Are you saying that she thought the same as me?' Maggie frowned.

'Yes, I believe she did,' Sam admitted. 'In fact, I'd go so far as to say she believed that right from the start— when she first came to the interview. I thought I'd made it plain to her that I wasn't interested, but obviously I hadn't made it plain enough. She came on quite strong as a matter of fact that Sunday when you came to St Rhadagund's and she was there—she said she was just passing. In the end I didn't think she was ever going to go. And then again at the bonfire party, she asked me for a lift home and then she clung to me like a limpet.'

'I thought…' Maggie swallowed.

'What did you think?'

'It doesn't matter…'

'No, tell me. Please.'

'I thought that night of the party that you and she…you and she had spent the night together.'

'Oh, Maggie.' Distractedly Sam ran a hand over his hair. 'That was the night when I dropped her off at her flat and I told her once and for all that there was nothing between us and that there never would be.'

Maggie stared at him. She'd been in torment that night, when all the time… 'Is that the only reason you had reservations about taking her on as practice manager?' she asked weakly at last.

Sam shrugged. 'Not entirely. I suppose it was also partly because of a hunch that she wouldn't fit in with the others. And I guess my hunch has proved correct. She doesn't fit in, does she?'

'Well, no,' Maggie admitted. 'I suppose she doesn't really.'

'Unfortunately she's trying to impose London procedures on a rural practice, and you know as well as I do that that doesn't work either with the staff or the patients. Imagine trying to tell poor old Percy or any of them really that they can't see their doctor for a week. They wouldn't accept it—they would quite simply park themselves in the waiting room until one of us was free, just as they've always done. I'm afraid Fiona has failed to grasp the fact that these people are our friends as well as our patients.'

'Maybe she'll learn in time,' said Maggie.

'We won't have the chance to find out.' Sam shook his head.

'Why?' Maggie frowned.

'I had a long talk with Fiona yesterday. I felt I had to try and sort things out after all the arguments at work otherwise we were in danger of losing all our reception staff.'

'And did you succeed?' asked Maggie quietly.

'Well, it wasn't easy,' he admitted.

'I can imagine,' said Maggie dryly. 'So how did you leave things with Fiona?' she asked slowly after a moment. Deep inside she was aware of a feeling of excitement, which was steadily mounting, but at the same time she was trying hard not to read too much into it because even though Sam had just confirmed that he had no feelings for Fiona, it didn't necessarily mean he had feelings for her.

'As regards the practice, I'm afraid we will be looking for another practice manager.'

'You didn't sack her!'

'No, of course not. I wouldn't take a decision like that without discussing it with you and Jon first. No, in the end I didn't have to do anything because Fiona announced that she intends handing in her notice first thing on Monday morning. She said her position in the practice had become untenable.'

'I see,' said Maggie slowly. She was silent for a moment, trying to take in what Sam had just said, then, looking up at him again tentatively, she said, 'Is that what you came here to tell me, Sam—that we no longer have a practice manager?'

'No, Maggie.' Sam shook his head. 'I didn't come here to talk about Fiona at all.' Raising his hand, he gently tilted her chin so that she was forced to look into his eyes. 'Have you really no idea why I'm here?'

In the silence that followed all that could be heard in

the room was the ticking of the old school clock on the wall and the gentle crackling of the pine log in the grate. 'No. You said you came to talk to me.' Maggie spoke at last. 'That you had something to tell me.'

'Yes,' Sam agreed. 'That's true. I came to tell you about this lady in my life. She's been there a long time, Maggie—first as a colleague and very dear friend but gradually she's come to mean more and more to me.'

'Have you told this lady how much she means to you?' asked Maggie. She was aware that while Sam had been speaking her heart had started beating rather faster than usual.

'Not yet,' Sam replied.

'Why not?'

'Well, the lady in question has been through a very tough time recently and I wasn't sure how she would react or even if she was ready to move on yet. I wasn't even sure whether she would look at me in that light or whether I would always simply be a friend and a colleague in her eyes.'

'Have you never showed even an inkling about the way you feel?' asked Maggie softly.

'I did try once,' Sam admitted, 'but she wasn't ready and I knew she hadn't even considered me as anything more than a friend. I was afraid of frightening her off so since then I've bided my time.'

'And how has this lady been since that time?'

'Well, for a while I thought we'd grown closer but lately there's been a coolness between us that I couldn't understand. Maybe now I know what that coolness was about but I didn't know before…and I couldn't bear it. That's why I'm here, Maggie. I can't wait any longer. I need to tell you how I feel about you and how much you mean to me. I'm sorry if it's too soon…but I can't help it…'

'Oh, Sam.' With a deep sigh Maggie put her arms around him and rubbed her face against the slightly rough texture of his sweater. 'Sam,' she whispered at last, 'it isn't too soon. Believe me, it isn't a moment too soon.'

'When did you know?' she murmured. It was later. She had made the tea and they were seated very close together on the sofa in front of the fire, Sam with one arm around Maggie's shoulders.

'That I was in love with you?' He considered for a moment. 'Some months ago,' he admitted at last. 'I've always been very, very fond of you, Maggie, but you know that. Then one day someone said they couldn't bear to think of you being alone for the rest of your life, and someone else—I think it might have been Jon—said something to the effect that a lovely lady like you would be bound to find someone else. It was then that I real- ised—and I have to say it hit me like a sledgehammer— that I didn't want you to find anyone else. I wanted you for myself.'

'But you didn't say anything… I had no idea.'

'I didn't dare say anything. It was too soon for you. I knew that. I knew I had to give you time. I knew you weren't ready, just as I knew that if I rushed you, I stood the chance of losing you for ever.'

'You're right,' she agreed. 'I wasn't ready then. I was more than happy to have your friendship and support, but I'd never considered anything else. But then that day on the beach with the children…'

'I know.' Sam nodded ruefully. 'I thought I'd blown it then, I really did. It wasn't planned, Maggie, really it wasn't. It just happened. Suddenly you were there in my arms, so close to me that I didn't want to let you go...'

'And I pushed you away. I'm so sorry, Sam, but at that point I was quite shocked—I suppose because the idea was completely alien to me. But I have to say the shock came as much from my own reaction. I enjoyed it, Sam. Just for a moment there, before I had time to think, I enjoyed being close to you... And afterwards, once the idea had been planted in my mind, I found myself thinking about it at all sorts of odd times.'

'I have to say your reaction that morning you thought I'd gone missing gave me fresh hope,' said Sam with a chuckle.

'My reaction made me think even more,' said Maggie. 'I think it was only then that I realised just how much you'd come to mean to me. The thought of life without you was quite simply more than I could bear. But you didn't make any further move and I even began to wonder whether you weren't able to trust anyone again after what happened with Claire.'

Sam gave a deep sigh. 'No, it wasn't that,' he said. 'I realise now that Claire and I should never have married in the first place. I knew about her earlier relationship with Luke but I suppose with the arrogance of youth I imagined it didn't matter. I can see now that Claire and Luke are two of a kind. I was hurt when she left me, or rather my pride was hurt, but it's over now and I can honestly say I don't feel any bitterness. No, the reason I made no further move was nothing to do with Claire. It was quite simply because I thought I'd overstepped the mark once and I was terrified of doing the same thing again and losing you completely.'

'And then,' Maggie went on after a while, 'when I thought you and Fiona were in a relationship...it hurt,

Sam, it honestly hurt. I kept asking myself how I'd cope if you and Fiona married and I had to see the two of you together every day for the rest of my working life, and the answer was, I didn't know. I really didn't know. It would have been like some sort of living nightmare.'

'Well, that's not going to happen...' his arm tightened protectively around her '...so you needn't give it another thought.'

'So what is going to happen?' Turning her head, she studied his profile.

'Whatever you'd like to happen. We can get married. We could embark on a torrid, passionate affair without telling anyone, or we could take things really slowly, one step at a time, which is what I'm prepared to do because ultimately I think that's what you'll want.'

'Oh, I don't know,' replied Maggie, considering. 'I quite liked the sound of the torrid affair...'

'You wanton hussy!' Sam turned and pulled her into his arms. The gesture was meant to be teasing but the situation changed when Sam looked deeply into her eyes then took her face between his hands and covered her mouth with his.

The kiss, long and passionate, sent shivers up and down Maggie's spine, stirring her desires and opening up a whole new realm of possibilities as their relationship moved into uncharted waters. This had been the one aspect that had bothered Maggie—that she knew Sam too well and that there was no element of mystery about their relationship—but as the passion flared inside her and her senses were aroused she knew she'd been wrong and that, far from knowing all there was to know about Sam, she really knew very little at all. She might have known all about Sam the doctor, or Sam the friend, but she knew nothing of Sam the lover, and as she sensed his own arousal she realised it was going to be quite wonderful finding out.

'So where will we live, your place or mine?'

It was the following day and Sam had brought his children over for Sunday lunch. He and Maggie had agreed the previous day that they would tell the children together. They were in the kitchen, enjoying a glass of wine while they waited for the joint of meat to cook, and they were watching the children who were outside in the garden, throwing sticks for the two dogs.

'I was wondering about that,' said Maggie in answer to Sam's question. 'Did you have anything in mind?'

'Well, St Rhadagund's would be more practical because it's larger, but I couldn't imagine you ever wanting to leave Mill House.'

'Oh, I don't know,' said Maggie, sipping her wine. 'I think I might be persuaded. There's something special about St Rhadagund's and you're right—we will need a lot more room. I like to think that Richard and Emma will come to stay even more often than they do at the moment…do you think Claire would allow that?'

'Yes, I think she would, especially now that I'm to be part of a family again. Richard wanted to come and live with me, you know.' Sam smiled. 'I doubt whether she'd allow that but she's been saying lately that she and Luke want to travel so it could suit everyone if the children came more often.'

'There would be room for Ingrid there as well, wouldn't there?' asked Maggie.

'Yes, there would,' Sam agreed. 'You think she would come?'

'Oh, I do hope so,' said Maggie. 'I would like to spend

more time with the children if I can—maybe I could go back to part time at the surgery.'

'I was hoping you'd say that.' Putting down his glass, Sam drew her into his arms. 'You work far too hard.'

'Whatever, we'll still need Ingrid,' said Maggie, winding her arms around Sam's neck. 'You know, I can still hardly believe this is happening.'

'I know,' he replied. 'It's like a dream. I only hope I don't wake up.'

As his mouth covered hers, so engrossed were they in each other that neither of them heard the kitchen door open and William come in from the garden.

'Mum,' he said, 'when's lunch? I'm absolutely starving.'

Sam and Maggie sprang guiltily apart and stared at William.

'Oh, darling,' said Maggie, hastily pushing back her hair. 'You weren't meant to see that. We were going to tell you when you were all together…'

'What, about you and Sam snogging?' William sniffed, his eyes lighting up as his gaze came to rest on the huge apple pie Ingrid had made. 'Oh, we knew all about that. We said it was about time the pair of you got married. Shall I call the others and tell them lunch is ready?'

'Yes, darling,' said Maggie weakly. 'I think you'd better.'

'So much for us wondering how to broach the subject and how they'd take it,' said Sam with a laugh as William went back into the garden.

'They never fail to amaze me,' said Maggie.

'It won't all be that easy,' warned Sam. 'You know all those stories we hear in the surgery about step-parents and stepchildren… I have to tell you, most of the time Richard lives in a world of his own and Emma likes her own way.'

'And I foresee all sorts of problems with Jessica when she's into make-up and boys... And we have the whole teenage thing to come yet with all four of them...' Maggie gave a little shudder. 'But at least now we'll be able to face all that together. I feel this is a new beginning for us all. A wonderful new beginning.'

Sam pulled her into his arms again. 'Do you think the children would notice if lunch was half an hour late?' he murmured against her hair.

'Well, Wills would,' she replied.

'How about ten minutes?'

'We might just get away with that,' she whispered with a little sigh as she lifted her face for his kiss.

Modern Romance™
...seduction and
passion guaranteed

Tender Romance™
...love affairs that
last a lifetime

Sensual Romance™
...sassy, sexy and
seductive

Blaze™
...sultry days and
steamy nights

Medical Romance™
...medical drama on
the pulse

Historical Romance™
...rich, vivid and
passionate

29 new titles every month.

*With all kinds of Romance for
every kind of mood...*

MILLS & BOON®

Makes any time special™

MAT4

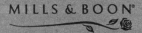

MILLS & BOON®

Medical Romance™

INNOCENT SECRET by Josie Metcalfe

Part 3 of Denison Memorial Hospital

Dr Joe Faraday is a man who keeps his heart hidden, and Nursing Sister Vicky Lawrence has her own secrets. She knows Joe wants her but something is holding him back. Vicky wonders if anything will tip him into her arms—and then her safety is put under threat...

HER DR WRIGHT by Meredith Webber

Dr Detective – Down Under

Rowena knew she was in love with her boss, Dr David Wright, and was beginning to suspect he felt the same. David was under suspicion for his wife's disappearance three years ago and Rowena desperately wanted to comfort him. But David refused to let her get involved—how could he offer her a future with his past hanging over him?

THE SURGEON'S LOVE-CHILD by Lilian Darcy

American surgeon Candace Fletcher feels the sizzling attraction as soon as Dr Steve Colton meets her off the plane in Australia—and the ensuing affair is passionate and intense. Then, just a few weeks before Candace is due to return home, the bombshell drops: she's pregnant!

On sale 1st March 2002

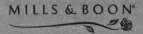

MILLS & BOON®

Medical Romance™

BACK IN HER BED *by Carol Wood*

Dr Alison Stewart ended her marriage to Sam when she accused him of having an affair, and he left for Australia. Now her determined husband is back, and the passion between them is still scorching. Sam is back in the marriage bed, but does Alison want him in her life forever?

THE FAMILY HE NEEDS *by Lucy Clark*

Reunited after ten years, it seems that surgeons Zac Carmichael and Julia Bolton are about to rekindle their relationship. But Zac's traumatic past means his instincts are to keep Julia, and her young son Edward, at a distance. Try as he might, however, he knows he can't just walk away from the family he needs…

THE CITY-GIRL DOCTOR *by Joanna Neil*

Suffering from a broken heart, Dr Jassie Radcliffe had left the city to join a challenging rural practice. Her new colleague, Dr Alex Beaufort, made it clear he didn't think she was up to the job, but secretly, he was impressed with Jassie. Then her ex-boyfriend turned up—just as Alex was falling in love with her!

On sale 1st March 2002

Available at most branches of WH Smith, Tesco, Martins, Borders, Eason, Sainsbury's and most good paperback bookshops. 0202/03b

Treat yourself this Mother's Day to the ultimate indulgence

3 brand new romance novels and a box of chocolates

= only £7.99

Available from 15th February

MIRANDA LEE

Secrets & Sins

revealed

SEDUCED BY HER BODYGUARD AND STALKED BY A STRANGER...

Available from 15th March 2002

Available at most branches of WH Smith,
Tesco, Martins, Borders, Eason, Sainsbury's
and most good paperback bookshops.

0402/35/MB34

FREE!

2 Books

and a surprise gift!

We would like to take this opportunity to thank you for reading this Mills & Boon® book by offering you the chance to take TWO more specially selected titles from the Medical Romance™ series absolutely FREE! We're also making this offer to introduce you to the benefits of the Reader Service™—

- ★ FREE home delivery
- ★ FREE gifts and competitions
- ★ FREE monthly Newsletter
- ★ Books available before they're in the shops
- ★ Exclusive Reader Service discount

Accepting these FREE books and gift places you under no obligation to buy; you may cancel at any time, even after receiving your free shipment. Simply complete your details below and return the entire page to the address below. ***You don't even need a stamp!***

YES! Please send me 2 free Medical Romance books and a surprise gift. I understand that unless you hear from me, I will receive 4 superb new titles every month for just £2.49 each, postage and packing free. I am under no obligation to purchase any books and may cancel my subscription at any time. The free books and gift will be mine to keep in any case.

M2ZEB

Ms/Mrs/Miss/Mr ....Initials ....
BLOCK CAPITALS PLEASE

Surname ....

Address...

....

....Postcode ....

Send this whole page to:
UK: The Reader Service, FREEPOST CN81, Croydon, CR9 3WZ
EIRE: The Reader Service, PO Box 4546, Kilcock, County Kildare (stamp required)